KING HUNT

A PERFECT PLAY NOVEL

LAYLA REYNE

LAYLA REYNE

ADRENALINE-FUELED ROMANCE

King Hunt

Copyright © 2023 by Layla Reyne

Cover Design: Cate Ashwood Designs

Cover Photography: Wander Aguiar Photography

Editing: Susie Selva

Proofreading: Lori Parks

First Edition

June, 2023

E-Book ISBN: 978-1-7373524-9-5

Paperback ISBN: 979-8-9869229-0-4

Content Warnings: Explicit sex; explicit language; violence; trafficking; off-page death of a former spouse; instances and/or discussion of homophobia, parental neglect, depression, and PTSD.

ABOUT THIS BOOK

When love is the only play that matters...

Agents Bishop and Marshall know:
The clock is ticking.
They control the most dangerous pieces on the board.
Sacrifices will be required to win the game.

Levi and Marsh need to:
Get home to each other and their son.
Fall asleep in each other's arms again.
Start living the happily ever after the rings on their fingers
promise.

What began as a marriage of convenience is now the rock
Marsh and Levi cling to as they enter the endgame.
But defeating two kings is no easy feat.
They'll have to make all the right moves and lure their
enemies to their side of the board, where they have the
advantage.

But winning may cost them everything—their careers, their lives, and the love that's become the center of their world.

King Hunt is the final book of the Perfect Play trilogy and should be read after Dead Draw and Bad Bishop. This swoony, single dad, marriage of convenience romance matches two mature, competent men and delivers the happily ever after they both so deeply deserve.

For all the readers who loved Marsh from first smirk and cheered him (and me) on to this HEA

ONE

"YOU NEED TO UNDERSTAND." Stefan Sanders's English was the definition of neutral. Trained, carefully spoken, no trace of an accent. Not from his Austrian heritage, not from his London schooling, not from his life in the States. A true chameleon. "This is a game between two chess masters, a father and the son he always wanted, seeing how far they can push each other and the world. I'm just a pawn. So are my parents and sister. So are you, Agent Marshall, and so is your husband, even if his last name is Bishop."

Marsh folded his arms and dug his fingers into his biceps, trying to ground himself, to keep his world from spinning apart. It had been three hours since his boss had charged into his hotel room, eight hours since his husband had taken Catherine Sanders into custody then boarded a train to Munich, nine hours since Marsh had last held Levi in his arms.

Yes, this had been their contingency plan, but the tilt-awhirl was no less dizzying because he understood the mechanics of it. He'd understood the how of the ride when he was a kid too. He'd only been able to tolerate it once his mother had taught him an old ballet trick. Focus on a single point while the world spun around him.

Focus.

On the hulking human trafficker across the interrogation table from him. Stefan looked equal parts tired and relieved, equal parts out of place in his rumpled tux—a clash with his crooked nose, scruffy beard, and colorful tattoos—and like he was born in one—his uncle one of the wealthiest men in the world. A criminal fronting as a phil-anthropist. And now serving as the war chest for a presidential hopeful.

"Exactly how far do Charles and Representative Anthony want to push the world?" Marsh asked.

"To war." Stefan's calm, matter-of-fact answer belied the death and destruction that had paved the road of Charles's and Stewart's long game. One they all, including Sophie, Stefan's lover and Marsh's late friend and mentor, had been caught up in too. "You know what my uncle does."

"He traffics people," Chief Inspector Wagner said from the chair beside Marsh.

"And weapons," Marsh added, the picture coming together in his head.

"And basic commodities," Stefan continued. "Food, water, medical supplies. My uncle's so-called humanitarian aid." He split a glance between Wagner and Marsh. "You're both smart enough to know what makes the price of all those things—people, weapons, and commodities—soar."

War.

Stefan was right. They both knew the awful truth, not only as law enforcement agents but also as military veterans. Marsh had served in the army, Wagner in the British RAF. Like most soldiers, they'd seen food and medical shipments go astray. Marsh, as a cyber officer, had overheard the sort of deals thieving warlords made in exchange for guns and skin. A tangled web his legat team had been unraveling for years. An investigation he'd roped Wagner into in Vienna before he'd taken the case to San Diego and landed right in Levi's path.

"So every move up until now," Marsh said, "has been to drive to that conclusion?"

"Eventually," Stefan said. "Immediately, Stewart provided documentation and supply, the shelter as cover. He got the good PR of being connected to a major philanthropic organization and his dirty work handled quietly."

"And if Stewart becomes president," Wagner said, "your uncle gets unfettered access to the US and the Oval Office."

"In return for the occasional false flag operation and 'messes' Stewart can clean up to look like a hero. More ammunition for their eventual war."

One parasite feeding off another, drawing others into their criminal conspiracy and destroying everything and everyone in their path. Including their family members. "You say Catherine's a pawn." Marsh brushed a thumb over the extra ring on his left hand. Too small for any of his other fingers, Levi's ring sat snug on his pinky, nestled next to its match. "Why not a queen?"

Stefan's laugh was as dark as the bags under his eyes. "We were the ones exposed. Charles stayed shielded behind the foundation while Catt and I committed his crimes. I moved the victims, and she moved the money."

Wagner leaned forward and rested his forearms on the metal interrogation table. "So let me get this straight." His Cockney accent was thicker than usual, drawn out by the long hours and the case that continued to crater his life. "You controlled the supply chain, Catherine controlled the funds flow, and you two were pawns?"

"My uncle controls the contacts. And us."

"By threatening your parents," Marsh said, "who we've rescued off the board for you."

"I hope so, and for that, I thank you." His tone lightened. "I have never felt relief like I did last night when you intercepted me at the gala." Then nosedived. "But it is hard to comprehend freedom after so many years under his thumb, and when his son"—he made air quotes as much as the handcuffs would allow—"may be the next president of the United States."

"One, you are not free," Marsh clarified. "You will be prosecuted for a long list of trafficking-related crimes."

"My parents will be free, and I will be too from any leverage my uncle had over me."

"Two," Marsh continued, "Stewart Anthony will not be the next US president." Stefan didn't look like he believed him, but Marsh was one hell of a chess player too. He'd been setting up this king hunt for three plus years, had critical pieces on the board he hadn't even moved yet, not to mention the pieces already in the middle. Pieces he was still assessing. "How much did Catherine care about your parents' safety?"

Stefan shrugged. "Hard to know. She used them as leverage over me, same as Uncle Charles."

"But now she's making her own moves," Wagner speculated.

"We were told about Stewart's announcement in advance. She read the writing on the wall, same as I did. We had to make our moves. They were escalating." He flicked a gaze to Marsh. "Speed chess, if you will, and if someone connected the dots and followed the trail of bodies and weapons back to him, he wouldn't hesitate to throw us under the bus. Muscle and launderers are replaceable."

Marsh considered Catherine's play last night and the avenues left open to her. "Your sister thinks she has other contacts to work."

"In London," Wagner said, following his train of thought. "Maybe elsewhere. Maybe she thinks she can work Charles's too."

"That's the part I don't know," Stefan said. "Never wanted to." He spread his hands. Grunted when they would only go so far in the cuffs. "I have enough blood on my hands." He laced his fingers and stared at them. "If I'd sunk further into hell, I would never be able to get my parents out. That's what mattered to *me*."

Marsh didn't miss the emphasis on his last word; the truth Stefan had dodged earlier. That no, Catherine likely didn't care nearly as much about their parents as Stefan did. It didn't excuse his crimes, the hell he'd put countless victims and families through, but he seemed to feel genuine regret and remorse for his actions. Catherine, however, hadn't seemed relieved that her parents had been saved last night. Hadn't seemed to care one bit. She'd been too wrapped up in vindictive anger that Charles and Stewart had lived. That Marsh and Levi, with Stefan's help, had foiled her murderous plan.

The same vengeful, would-be murderess Marsh had sent his husband off into the world with that morning. He'd hang his head in his hands if it weren't for the criminal across the table and the colleagues watching from behind the observation glass. He straightened, snagged the legal pad from the corner of the table, and tossed it and a pen in front of Stefan. "Give us a list of where she's most likely to go in Munich and London and any likely stops in between."

While Stefan scribbled his list, Marsh followed Wagner out of the room. Special Agent Binu Patel, Marsh's current boss, pounced as soon as Marsh closed the door. "This is what Sophie knew. Why she was working him."

Yes, but Marsh suspected Sophie was also in love with Stefan. His late legat was the patron saint of lost causes. She'd tucked Sean and Marsh into her team, eased their transitions into the FBI, and nursed their broken hearts with friendship and enough work to keep them relatively distracted. Stefan with all his conflict, with his sad eyes and broken nose, with his steadfast devotion to his parents and his connections to the international criminals Sophie had been chasing for years, was the holy grail. They needed to go back through Sophie's files in light of all they'd learned the past twenty-four hours. Maybe on the flight to London because Marsh would bet the ring on his pinky that's where Levi and Catherine were headed.

"Marsh?" Binny snapped. "Are you listening to me?"

"I think," Sean said as he stepped to Marsh's side, "maybe we should adjourn for a few hours."

Binny opened his mouth to protest, and Julia stepped to Marsh's other side. "Levi and Catherine are under constant surveillance. We're tracking their every move."

"We know where Charles and Anthony are too," Ross

added. "Give us a few hours to shower and caffeinate, then let's regroup."

"And maybe by then," Wagner said, "Levi will have more information for us too."

Hell, Marsh would just settle for an I'm-still-alive text.

TWO

TEN MINUTES and a list from Stefan later, Marsh was sliding into the back seat of Sean's rented SUV. They were a mile out from the station when Julia twisted in the passenger seat to look back at him. "Have you heard from Levi?"

In the ever-changing world of people he could trust, the only two people on the current scene Marsh trusted completely were the two in the car with him. He withdrew his phone from his pocket and opened his encrypted chat app, toggling to the one with Levi. "Nothing." He closed the app and set the phone aside, facedown on the seat. "They must still be on the move." He and Levi had agreed to minimal contact until Levi knew they would be stationary long enough for Marsh to catch up.

"Do you think they'll go all the way to London today?" Sean asked.

"It's possible. They started early enough."

"I'll alert the pilot as soon as we get back to the hotel."

Sean drummed his fingers on the wheel. "We'll be ready to go as soon as we get word."

Julia righted herself in the seat. "Catherine wouldn't have made that play last night if she didn't have better control of the funds than we know."

"And contacts," Marsh said. "She'll make stops along the way to shore those up." Assuming she and Levi weren't stopped first. "Any word from DOJ yet?"

"Cam took care of our reinstatements and the provisional custody paperwork," Julia confirmed. "FBI took custody of Catherine Sanders, pending extradition. The Federal Police will retain custody of Stefan Sanders."

The deal stung, but they'd had to make it. He and Levi had been chasing the Eder Capital facilitator—Stefan—for months. But Stefan was out of the game now. Wagner and Ross could pump him for info as they needed, but he wasn't a piece to match up against the power players.

"Per Charlie," Julia said, "extradition paperwork will be reviewed first thing, DC morning."

Marsh glanced at his watch. Five hours for Levi's actions to be officially sanctioned. Five hours for shit to go sideways.

Sean's blue gaze snagged his in the rearview mirror. "We've got eyes on him," he said, correctly reading Marsh's tension. "And Levi's got eyes on Catherine. We could have lost her completely if you and Levi hadn't made your move."

Marsh sank back into his chair, last night's curveball replaying in his head.

"It can't be morning yet." Levi tossed an arm over Marsh's waist and snuggled against his back. "Turn off the alarm."

Marsh flung out an arm the direction of the offending noise, but before he could reach the phone, it mercifully silenced itself.

Which his alarm would not do.

It rang again, the screen lighting up the dark room.

Levi immediately tensed, the same realization striking him. "Whose phone?"

"Mine." *Marsh stretched for the bedside table and plucked his phone off the charger. Wagner's name lit the screen. He answered the call and flipped it to speaker.* "Wags, what's going on?"

"Catherine will make bail within the hour."

"Bail?" *Levi shot up beside him.* "When was it set? It's the middle of the night."

"Her lover, the minister of interior, pulled some strings. She's going to be released into his custody."

"They'll run," *Marsh said.*

"No shit," *Wagner replied.* "I can tie things up in paperwork long enough for you to get down here."

"We're on our way." *Marsh ended the call and tossed his phone back on the table. So much for their reprieve.*

Levi's rough and ragged words shattered the peace for good. "You know you can't come with me."

"I know." *They had planned for this potential turn of events; a contingency they'd been prepared to exercise. Catherine seemed to genuinely like Levi. If there was anyone who could turn her, it was Levi, but in order to do so, he needed to go it alone, at least to start. Alone left Levi the most options for how to play this with Catherine, how to move her into the position they needed. Professionally, Marsh got it, but personally, it didn't make it hurt any less. Sending his other half into danger was still sending his other half into danger. And without having his back, breaking promises he'd sworn to keep.* "It's just..." *Marsh flitted his hand, the one with the ring on it.* "We're partners."

In every sense of the word.

Levi caught his flailing hand and laced their fingers together. "Funny how that happened so fast." He lifted their joined hands and kissed the back of Marsh's. "Trust your partner. Your husband. I can handle this."

He whipped his gaze to the side, gaze clashing with the determined blue one that was so close. "I do, completely. You are the best agent I've ever worked with. But you're also my husband. The last thing I want to do is let you walk out that door alone."

Levi leaned forward and kissed him softly, lips brushing as he spoke. As he made his own promise. "I will bring my heart home to you."

It had been a mad dash after that, the two of them quickly showering and dressing, and Levi packing his go-bag. The hardest part had been watching Levi take off his wedding ring and set it atop the gala invite on the vanity. Right before he'd shoved Marsh against the wall and kissed him to within an inch of his life, everything they'd built together the last five weeks, the love that had taken hold and grown beyond their wildest imaginations, driving the kiss higher and higher, leaving them breathless.

After, Marsh had retrieved the ring and picked up the invite, turning it over and reading the two words Levi had scribbled on the back.

King Hunt.

They were on the same wavelength, personally and professionally. They could do this. Even if slipping Levi's ring on his pinky for safekeeping had felt like a knife to his heart. Nine hours later, it was the only thing holding him together.

The back seat door opened. "You okay?" Sean asked, voice pitched with concern.

"Just missing him." He mustered a small smile, grabbed his hat, and slid out of the car. "I suppose you know how that feels."

"Times two," Sean said with a wink. He shut the car door, then clasped Marsh's shoulder, his expression gentle and earnest. "It's the worst feeling in the world to be apart from them and also the best because you know how much this"—he tapped his chest over his heart—"is capable of."

More than Marsh had ever thought possible, and he would do whatever it took to bring his husband home. To make sure they both kept their promises.

THREE

LEVI SAT ALONE at a pub table in Karlsruhe, sipping a pilsner and picking at a plate of fries, wishing like hell Catherine had taken a liking to Marsh instead of him because at least Marsh would understand the conversation going on behind Levi. The third such conversation Catherine had had today.

One on the train from Salzburg to Munich with a person Levi had at first mistaken for a random college kid, the twentysomething in a hoodie, jeans, and backpack plopping down into the seat next to Catherine. But as soon as the ticket checker had passed, oddly without ever checking their tickets or passports, Catherine and the young person had begun conversing in rapid-fire German, a cell changing hands that Catherine seemed to think Levi hadn't noticed. Thirty minutes later, the kid stood, left the backpack behind, and disappeared into the next car. Catherine had made a beeline to the bathroom, changed into a knit dress and cardigan, and returned without the backpack.

In Munich, she'd strolled through the botanical gardens with an older woman, the two of them arm in arm, sipping coffee and sharing words Levi wouldn't understand much less hear from the distance he was tailing them. They'd parted once the morning sun was shining bright, and Catherine had met Levi back at the statue of Neptune, commending him on the distance he'd kept, her colleague oblivious to his presence.

From there, they'd taken another train to Karlsruhe, a town Levi had never heard of before today but that felt oddly familiar. Maybe because the pub he found himself in was so much like the one Marsh had taken him to in Vienna. Subterranean, a space that should be claustrophobic but that leaned more toward cozy, a bar stretching the length of one wall, the rest of the area filled with long tables and big booths. A single bartender served the handful of occupied stools and tables. Not too many this time of day. Perfect for whatever clandestine meeting Catherine was conducting with the man and woman in the booth behind Levi.

Catherine's tinkling laugh floated on the ale-scented air, she and the couple chatting like old friends. While Levi didn't understand most of what they said, he did recognize when pleasantries were over and the conversation shifted to business. Voices lowered, their words were harder to understand, but Levi didn't have to wonder about the names of people and places that reached his ears and the words that were close enough to English to guess.

Charles and Stewart.

Politics and Washington.

Transporting waren, which Levi thought must mean

something—people or guns—that Catherine wanted to traffic.

San Diego and Texas.

Every hair on Levi's arms rose. Was Catherine targeting his family? His colleagues? He strained to hear over his pounding pulse, over the blood rushing in his ears, listening for any mention of his name, David's, Marsh's, or any of their family members or colleagues. He struggled not to spin and defend, not to demand they speak English so he could understand what they were saying, not to pull out his phone and call Marsh and tell him to get everyone to safety. He white-knuckled his stein until the conversation moved on, Catherine and her associates speaking of other destinations, their focus still on the waren. Levi's panic waned and understanding dawned. With it a better idea of what Catherine was up to, what she'd been up to this entire day. Fuck, if he was right, Catherine was already halfway to doing what he and Marsh needed her to do in order to flush out Charles.

He waited for her associates to leave and for Catherine to slide into the chair across from him before leveling his hypothesis. "You're making a play for your uncle's trafficking routes. The ones west of the Mississippi."

She snagged a fry off his plate. "He'll need to shed assets while his pet is running for president."

"Assets." Levi scoffed. "Criminal enterprises, you mean." She didn't dispute him, just flitted her fingers in a dismissive gesture. "You think he's just going to let you take them?"

"It's not like he can get into a territorial fight with the spotlight on him." She gathered her auburn hair into a ponytail, using a hairband she pulled from her purse. She instantly looked years younger, a riotous conflict with her cutthroat words. "I should thank Stewart next time I see him. And your husband."

Levi barely stopped his thumb from brushing over the spot where his ring should be. "You do realize you're on your way to jail?"

Catherine's green eyes danced with amusement. "You do realize jail rarely stops criminal enterprises?"

"How long have you been planning this?"

"Well, it's not exactly what I'd planned." She lifted a hand to call the server over and ordered two glasses of scotch. The brief pause in their back-and-forth gave Levi a moment to recalibrate the day. To reconsider her maneuvers and reach another conclusion. He waited for the drinks to arrive, then leaned forward, twirling his glass between his fingers. "These are your contacts. You're setting up your own criminal enterprise. To rival his routes."

"Little bit of both." She eyed him over the rim of her glass. "And I've got all this time to do so before I go to jail, thanks to you and the minister."

It was a calculated play on her part. How much could she get away with while Levi and Marsh bought time and worked their angles? But where did Catherine see her play going in the long run? "What happens after Stewart wins— or more likely loses—the presidency?" Levi asked. "Assuming he even gets his party's nomination. Do you think your uncle will just let you keep those assets? Let you steal the routes right out from under his nose?" He sat back in his chair and sipped his scotch. "Whatever you think you have, it's temporary."

"Are you proposing to make it more permanent?"

All this was a calculated play on his and Marsh's part too. How much of the Catherine-induced chaos could they rein back in? Would there still be pieces left on the board by the time they were back on US soil? Or would the board be blown to bits?

Levi tossed back the rest of his scotch, burning away those doubts. He'd asked Marsh to trust him; Levi had to trust Marsh too. Had to trust their play would work, that Marsh would work his angles while Levi worked his. That with Marsh as his partner, he might finally fucking win at chess. He lowered the empty glass to the table. "Your brother and your parents will testify against your uncle. That's supply chain and explosives. You can tie Charles and Eder Capital directly to the money."

"You're so sure I control the money."

"You do or you wouldn't have gotten any of those meetings today. Still not sure how you're going to launder it now that we blew up your bitcoin scheme, but we'll figure it out."

She sipped her scotch and smiled. "I think you might be smarter than your husband. It took his team years to get this close, and you've been on the case how long?"

"We're this close because your partners at Orchard made a tactical error right under my nose and a bitcoin one right under Marsh's." Not to mention the ill-timed mistake she'd made to accelerate matters at the gala. "Are you sure there won't be more mistakes?"

Her pale cheeks flushed, understanding the mistakes he spoke of and those he didn't. She finished her scotch and checked her watch. "You've got the train to Paris, then to

London to convince me you and your partner and the inside of a jail cell are a better deal." She stood and shouldered her bag. "Tick tock, Agent Bishop."

Tick tock was right, but if he was on the clock, so was Catherine. And they were all running out of time.

FOUR

MARSH TRUDGED into his hotel room, tossed his Stetson on the chest of drawers, and fell back onto the bed. He stared at the ceiling and idly considered undressing, but the mere thought of righting himself and bending over to remove his boots sounded like the worst kind of torture. He closed his eyes instead and drifted on the edge of sleep, body too tired for more, mind too keyed up to shut down, heart aching for the warm body he'd gotten used to having beside him.

What were the chances he'd crawl into bed with Levi tonight? Slim. He wouldn't go so far as to say none—nothing about this case had been predictable—but realistically, he'd be lucky to share the same bed with Levi again this week. Who knew how long it would take for Catherine to make her move, for him and Levi to snare her in her own web, for Charles and Stewart to get caught in it too. As long as it needed to take. That was the right answer, even if Marsh didn't like it one bit. After five weeks under the same roof with Levi, the past two sharing a bed, the thought of one night without Levi tucked against him made Marsh's heart hurt.

He brushed his thumb over their rings. Five weeks. Five weeks for his world to be turned upside down, for life to give him everything he'd ever wanted only to have the goal post moved out of reach, his fairy-tale future paused pending the outcome of one final drive.

A drive he had to win. And lying in bed, failing to sleep, wasn't the way to do it. He had four hours until their scheduled debrief with Charlie's team. Enough time to start running searches, to pack the rest of his and Levi's things, then maybe he'd be tired enough to catch a nap. He dragged himself out of bed, retrieved his glasses and laptop, and got to work, identifying all the major rail routes between Munich and London with first-class service because Catherine was the sort who wouldn't travel in less. With no direct route, he took an educated guess at transfer points where she would have contacts and set up searches for her known associates in those locations. He wanted to be prepared with a list when Levi checked in, ready to iden-tify anyone he described and why Catherine may have met with them. Those searches running, he started back through their team's case notes, looking for other evidence and means of money laundering. If Catherine still had control of Eder's money, which as the banker of the bunch he bet she did, even after the stunt she pulled, they needed to sort how she'd keep EC's illegal operations funded now that the bitcoin scheme had been burned.

He was jotting down his notes—an organized crime list for Charlie and her SAC, Sutton Conder, to follow up on, a list for Ross and Binny of known launderers in Europe who'd had contact with any of the Sanders family, and a list for Wags of Austrian account numbers he would begin tracing first thing Monday morning—when his phone rang. He lunged for the device, heart in his throat, Levi's voice the thing he wanted most in the world. He glanced at the screen, and his stomach sank the opposite direction, dragging his heart with it.

David.

Their call with Levi's son was usually later in the day, at a decent hour Texas time. Not predawn at Mi Herencia. So why was David calling now? Was something wrong? How was Marsh going to explain Levi's absence? Marsh had anticipated having more time to prepare for this.

"Don't lie to him," Levi had said as he'd packed his go-bag. "I promised Kristin to always tell him the truth, and I've managed to keep that promise for two years. We're not gonna break it now."

Levi's "we" had been a bright spot in the swirling darkness. He was bringing Marsh all the way into the fold of his family, trusting him with his son and this important part of his late wife's legacy. But now, fuck, Marsh wondered how Levi had kept that promise.

The ringing stopped, and Marsh cursed. Sure, he could let it go to voicemail for now and wait for David to call back later, hopefully when Marsh had a better idea where Levi was and when they'd all be home again, but that felt suspiciously like lying. Marsh wouldn't be the one to betray Kristin either. He stood, tossed his glasses on the desk, and made his way out to the balcony. He leaned against the metal rail and gazed across the river at the charming town he and Levi had admired the day before, had talked about bringing David back to visit. He believed they would get that chance one day. Had to for the call he needed to make.

David answered on the first ring. "Is Dad's phone dead? It's going straight to voicemail." He didn't give Marsh a chance to reply, launching right into conversation, which, as the teen had come out of his shell, Marsh had realized was often his way. "Irina got called out to an emergency in Fort Davis and said if we got done early enough we could go to McDonald Observatory. Camilla said I should call before we left so you're not worried if I'm late calling tonight. But Dad's not picking up, so I'm calling you."

Marsh smiled, his heart warming even as it wobbled. David had fit so well into his family too. His moms had taken David in like the grandson they'd always wanted. "He's probably got his phone turned off."

"Oh shit!"

"Language."

David ignored him, same as he usually did when Levi made similar corrections. "Are y'all right in the middle of a work something?"

"He's working, yes."

David's quiet breathing was the only sound on the other end of the line.

"You there, David?"

His breath hitched, and his voice, when he spoke again, had a wobble in it similar to the one in Marsh's heart. "He's not with you."

"Listen, David."

The wobble escalated into high-pitched trembles. "Why's he not with you?"

"David, I need you to breathe and turn on your video." He sent through the video request, and a moment later, David appeared on-screen. His initial sunburn was giving way to flaked skin and more freckles, and his red curls looked like they hadn't seen a brush in days. Not that it would matter under the cowboy hat perched on the stall post behind him in what Marsh recognized was the surgical barn. "How're Kristin and Bond?" He asked after the baby goats, aiming to distract, to center David back in the here and now.

His expression hardened, a reappearance of the surly teen that had receded as of late. "I don't want to talk about them."

"David," he coaxed, "how are the kids? What's their weight up to?"

He huffed and rolled his eyes. So much like his dad. Marsh smiled as his heart gave another thump. Smiled wider as David rattled off an update on each baby goat.

"That all sounds good."

"Your stepmom is good at what she does."

An opening. Marsh took it. "So is your father." David shot him a green-eyed glare, and Marsh chuckled. "Feel better now?" Chuckled more as David flipped him off with a small smile of his own. "Listen to me, David. Yes, your father is flying solo." He kept going before the panic reddening David's cheeks worsened. "For a short time. But this is going exactly as we planned. Your dad is smart. The smartest person I've ever known. He's doing what he does best, and we have to trust him to handle himself. Look at all he's handled the past two years."

"He wasn't doing it well, not alone."

"And he's not alone now. I may not be with him, but I have his back. And yours."

"You're not supposed to let him get hurt."

"I will do everything in my power to keep that promise."

David slumped back against a stall door and snagged the hat off the post, twirling it around one fist, looking anywhere but at Marsh. "You won't leave us when this is over?"

"David, look at me." He waited for the green eyes to lift. Swallowed around the lump in his throat at the fear and worry there. He held up his left hand so David could see his and Levi's rings. He wriggled his pinky finger. "The only place this ring is going is back on your dad's finger." Wriggled his ring finger. "And mine's not going anywhere either. I'm not going to leave either one of you."

David bit one corner of his lip. Bit back the hope that flickered in his eyes. "Why?"

Marsh stoked that tiny ember with the truth he'd promised Levi. "Because I'm in love with your father. And I might even love you too."

David let his lip go, let a smile loose too, and a big breath later, flipped the hat up onto his head. "I just miss him. And you. I love it here, but I want to go home with you and Dad."

"There's nothing your father and I want more." Marsh pushed off the balcony rail and turned for the inside. To get back to work. "We'll make it happen, David, as soon as we can."

FIVE

"DID YOU GET ANY ACTUAL REST?" Sean asked as Marsh closed the door of the presidential suite behind him.

"About an hour." His eyes had eventually said no more and the rest of his body had likewise given him the middle finger. But the respite had been short-lived, his subconscious feeding him nightmares of David, cheeks wet and eyes red-rimmed, standing over a grave with the rest of the Bishop-Morelli clan behind him. Marsh had jolted awake before seeing the headstone, but his racing heart, knotted stomach, and clammy skin told him all he needed to know. Freaked him out enough to call it quits on the whole sleep thing. "I'll try again on the plane."

"Does that mean you don't want any of this?" Julia, in the adjacent kitchenette, lifted the coffee pot. "Time's short for the good shit. Back to American swill before you know it."

He liked her optimism. "Biggest mug you got." He flipped the dining chair to Sean's left around and straddled it backward, the better to hold up his tired body.

"Do we know where we're headed?" Sean asked.

He shook his head. "Still waiting for Levi to confirm their final destination. Surveillance last reported them in a Karlsruhe pub near the train station."

"So likely moving again." Julia passed out coffee mugs and slid into the chair across from Marsh. "You still think they're headed to London?"

"Pretty sure," he answered. "From Karlsruhe, they can catch the high-speed rail to Paris, then the Eurostar to London." Add the prior leg from Munich to Karlsruhe, and it was the route Marsh had suspected was the most likely. Fast and in style, probably on trains Catherine rode frequently, probably with staff who knew her well and would assume all was status quo with their frequent traveler. Who would never guess she was a wanted fugitive.

Sean's laptop chirped. "That'll be Charlie." He set aside his mug as the call connected and Charlie appeared on-screen. A soft, eager smile stretched across Sean's face, the same head-over-heels one Marsh had first seen on his best friend's face in Hanover last year. "Hey, babe."

"Hey, yourself." They held each other's gazes for several long seconds before Charlie seemed to reluctantly tear hers away to nod a greeting to Marsh and Julia. She was in yesterday's blazer, a new top on underneath, with her dark hair pulled up in a messy bun. Marsh doubted she'd left the office.

Sean, the sometimes idiot, said as much. "You look like you got about as much sleep as we did."

Julia swatted his shoulder. "Did you learn nothing at Emmitt Marshall charm school?"

"Ha!" Marsh scoffed. "You admit it! I am charming!"

"I'm sorry," Sean beseeched while Marsh and Julia

airplane food," Levi said. "And rail travel is a hell of a lot less hassle too. I wish we had these options in the States."

"Enjoy them while you're in Europe," the server said with a wink before retreating.

Catherine leaned forward, whispering conspiratorially, "You have a fan."

"I also have a husband."

She tilted her auburn top knot toward the server. "He doesn't know that." Tilted her glass toward herself as she eyed his left hand. "I don't know that."

He went to spin his ring and cringed at finding his finger bare, that ache in his chest making itself known again. He'd not worn it long, but being without it felt wrong, even if its absence was necessary. He and Marsh hadn't known which angles they'd need to play with Catherine, so they'd agreed to keep them all open, including the one Levi least wanted to play. Hadn't had to yet. Was that what Catherine was hinting at now?

In any event, she swerved a different direction. "I take it from your exchange with the rail authority just now and on the train to Paris that Marsh got you whatever paperwork you needed to extradite me."

"He did."

"You know, once we get to London, we can just disappear." And swerved back onto the road Levi did not want to travel. She spun a lock of hair around a finger and sipped her champagne, eyeing him over the rim of her glass. Maybe it was the lack of sleep, maybe it was the intelligence he'd seen on display all day, whatever it was, Levi rolled his eyes and chuckled at the show. Similar to the server, Catherine didn't seem the least bit offended. She dropped the sultry act and let loose an easy, relaxed smile. She grabbed another piece of cheese and rested back in her seat, nibbling. "I knew the second you two walked into my office that you were head over heels in love with your husband."

"Then why continue to try and lure me to your side?"

"Because love can't be all there is. And because you hadn't picked a side between me and my uncle."

He could argue her first point on love, could point to a dozen examples where love had overcome impossible odds —his parents, Marsh's mothers, their friends, him and Marsh—but what he'd said to Marsh and Sean in Vienna last week rang again in his ears. *Most rich people think they can buy anyone. They think other people just want to be rich too.* That was the angle he'd rather play. The one that intersected with her second point, which Levi had been noodling all day. He leaned forward and buttered a hunk of baguette. He savored it while mentally debating his approach, finally settling on, "You don't actually want your uncle's approval, do you?"

"I just want his empire."

But that wasn't exactly right either, was it? "His or your own?" he asked. "At first, I thought this was about you wanting to be the rightful heir. You didn't like being third in line behind Stewart and Stefan. But after Salzburg, I think you just want them all out of your way, and you don't even need his contacts. You've got your own."

"Well, I want some of them." She finished her champagne, set the glass back on the table, and swiped another piece of cheese. "But yes, I just need his transit lanes. Or better ones."

Something Marsh had said earlier now rang along with his own words, spurring another idea he'd have to discuss with Marsh and the team in London. In the meantime, he drew the champagne bottle out of the bucket and refilled Catherine's glass. "Why are you telling me all this?"

"Because you picked a side. *Mine.* And now I know your husband will follow your lead. Anywhere."

He finally picked up his own glass and tilted it in acknowledgment. She'd been playing her own angle too. Expertly. No doubt he and Marsh were playing a dangerous game, letting Catherine move around the board relatively unchecked. It was a calculated risk, aimed at taking down the bigger threats at checkmate. But Catherine was on the clock too with limited time to make her moves. He gave her a little more space to maneuver. "Our flight leaves Heathrow at ten. We're at the Sofitel Heathrow until then."

"Under surveillance?"

He drained his glass. "You bet."

She laughed and dove for the last hunk of cheese. "I can work with that."

SEVEN

IT WAS past midnight when Levi and Catherine arrived in London. Wouldn't know it, though, by the boisterous crowd at the hotel bar, a group that grew louder when they spied Catherine at the reception desk. Glasses and cheers were raised, a champagne bottle popped, and two of the group broke off, laughing and stumbling their direction. "This is the opposite of clandestine," Levi said as they crossed the lobby toward the bar.

"It's not supposed to be," Catherine replied. "If this is my last night of freedom, I want to spend it with my friends."

"Do your friends know what you do for a living?"

"Work as an investment banker and run my family's foundation?" She grinned, that Cheshire cat one she'd worn the first day he, Marsh, and Sean had walked into EC headquarters. "Of course they do." She snatched one of the keys from his hand, then strode ahead of him into the bar, the arm not tugging her suitcase outstretched, open for the friends who barreled into her. She curled them into a hug,

EIGHT

SEAN OPENED the hotel room door, and Levi's face fell. Marsh debated revoking Sean's best friend card right there on the spot. Didn't matter that it had been Marsh's idea to have him answer and also Marsh's idea to stand on the opposite side of the room. If he'd opened the door to his husband, Marsh would have done a half dozen indecent things in front of their colleagues. Judging by Levi's expression in that split second before it fell, when his hungry, blue gaze had clashed with Marsh's, he was ready to do the same half dozen indecent things. Maybe more. So yeah, Marsh had been right to stand out of reach.

Unfortunately for Levi, doing so put him directly in Binny's line of fire. Levi had barely closed the door behind him when Marsh's boss launched into the tirade he'd been on since he'd barreled into their Salzburg hotel room earlier that—now yesterday—morning. "I already told your husband this, and I'll tell you too. That's the last time you pull a stunt like this without first clearing it with our legat office."

Levi dropped his bag on the floor then straightened to his full height, tall enough to meet Marsh's gaze again over Binny's shoulder. "How long is the flight to DC?"

"Eight hours," Marsh answered.

"And takeoff is still at ten?"

"Correct."

Levi shifted his attention back to Binny. "All right."

"Good," Binny said with a nod.

"All right," Levi repeated, then qualified. "For the next seventeen hours."

Marsh did the math in his head. Levi was giving Binny the hours between now and takeoff, plus the flight time. But that was all. And Binny, fueled by too much caffeine, a list of demands from Justice, and God only knew what off-book intelligence his brother Ajay was feeding him, didn't like it one bit. "The US won't be the only country that wants to charge her. We just got there first, and we had to give up Stefan Sanders to do it. This is a delicate, diplomatic situation."

"She's in our custody," Levi said. "With an extradition order you signed. Do I need to pull out my phone and show it to you again?"

Snarky Levi was not helping Marsh tamp down the desire to leapfrog Binny and tackle-kiss his husband. Levi was putting off the same tired and grumpy vibes he had that night in the restaurant when Marsh had proposed. All he'd wanted to do then—and now—was to make it better for the beautiful man. Five weeks, a wedding band, and a heart roped later, the urge was only stronger.

"I signed off, *after* you'd already gone over my head, because Marsh said the intel would be worth it."

Levi's gaze skated back to Marsh's, one corner of his mouth hitched. "Making promises on my behalf?"

He winked, returning some of the torture. "Because I know you're the best."

Binny shifted so he could split a glare between them. "You two have got to start taking this seriously."

That was a push too far for Marsh. He paused his need to jump his husband and defended him instead. "What the hell do you think we've been doing the past five weeks?"

"Or the past twenty-four hours?" Levi added, similarly on the defensive. He stepped closer to Binny, color rising in his pale cheeks, making the bags under his eyes more pronounced. "I'd much rather be home in San Diego with Marsh and our son, but I've spent the past day making nice with a fucking murderer while trailing her around Europe. All to get you and this team intel. So don't tell me to start taking this fucking seriously."

Marsh would've stepped between them, would've tried to defuse the situation, but Levi's "our son" froze him in place. He'd begun to feel that way about David, thought Levi did too from the future plans they'd been making, but to hear him say it, for it to fall so casually from his lips like it was a given, made Marsh's heart swell. Made it feel like it would explode from all the hope and love Levi had packed into it the past five weeks.

Thrown as he was, words caught somewhere behind a too big heart and the too big lump in his throat, Marsh looked to Julia for the save. She knew him well enough to pick up the ball. "Agent Bishop," she called in her major-turned-ASAC voice. She waved him over to the table. "Come tell us what you've learned."

Levi dead-eyed Binny another moment before turning toward the table. "Ma'am."

"I'm going to chalk that 'ma'am' up to not enough sleep. And it's Julia now. I'm not taking Kwan as an answer either."

"Thank you, Julia." He chuckled, some of the tension receding from his frame, more of the weariness making itself known as he slumped into the chair next to the open one behind Marsh's laptop.

"You coming, Nerd?" Julia said.

Marsh unstuck himself and slid into the chair beside Levi. His ass had barely hit the seat when Levi claimed his left hand and slid the wedding band off Marsh's pinky. He slid it back onto his ring finger and made a fist, nestling the ring where it belonged. "Turns out I didn't need to take this off. Catherine saw right through me."

Marsh should've been worried, but pride and gratitude won out. His ring on such an incredible man's finger was a sight he would never tire of. Levi's presence at his side was something he would never tire of either. The relief he felt at having him back there sank deep down to his bones, settling him for the first time all day.

Binny, the asshole, poked the peaceful bubble. "So you didn't get the intel?"

"I didn't say that." Levi shifted closer to Marsh, cementing the renewed bond even as they got down to business. "Catherine had three meetings. I didn't catch names, but I can describe each person and exactly where we met them. She was friendly and familiar with all, so I'd say we're looking for known associates."

"I've already compiled lists based on your stops," Marsh said.

Sean tapped his toe against the boxes on the floor between him and Julia. "We'll also check in the case files."

"Add Binny's Europol and other connections"—translation: Ajay—"and we should be able to make quick work of things." Marsh couldn't afford for this to take all night. Thinking positively, he and Levi would be in DC together tomorrow, then on their way home shortly thereafter. Thinking realistically, they didn't know how long the next phase of their plan would take to play out. He had to bank every minute he could with Levi so he could make it through the hours—possibly days—without him.

Binny, temporarily appeased now that there was intel to act on, settled into the seat across from them and drew his laptop closer. "The first contact was in Munich?"

"Before that actually," Levi answered, then described the person who had sat beside Catherine on the train from Salzburg to Munich.

"Were the phone and change of clothes the primary purpose of that meet?" Julia asked while Marsh searched his lists, Binny his databases, and Sean their files.

"I don't think so," Levi said. "If it had been, the contact would have left the bag and moved on. They wouldn't have sat and talked to Catherine."

"Less obvious maybe," Marsh said, playing devil's advocate because he tended to agree with Levi. There was likely more to that meet.

"Maybe," Levi conceded. "But I don't think so."

"Why did they hand the phone to her instead of just leaving it in the bag?" Sean asked.

"Biometrics," Binny answered. "They both had to touch it at the same time for Catherine to be able to unlock it. Means we likely won't be able to lift and bug it. We've seen the tech in some of the more advanced devices lately. It's a favorite of paranoid executives and terrorist cells."

"That's frightening." Marsh mumbled his first reaction, then quickly on its heels, his second. "And helpful." He filtered his Salzburg and Munich lists further, which brought the potential identities of their person of interest down to fourteen. He nudged the laptop in front of Levi.

He scrolled through them, then shook his head. "None of those."

"Any chance you made a Vienna list?" Sean asked.

"I did," Marsh replied. "Why?"

Sean dropped a folder onto the table, open to a black-and-white surveillance photo. "This is from our files on the U-Bahn bomber, Peter Bauer. Is that your person?" he asked Levi.

One look and Levi nodded. "That's them."

"Let me reapply the filters," Marsh said. "Binny, can you run facial recognition?"

"On it." He drew the photo to his side of the table, snapped a photo with his phone that he dropped to his computer, then began furiously clicking and typing. He could be a prickly son of a bitch, but he was a good agent, and when his relentlessness was properly directed, one of the most productive Marsh had worked with.

"Go on with the others," Marsh said. "These searches will run in the background."

Levi next filled them in on the older woman in Munich, who was easily identified. Bethany Futch was Catherine's mentor from the London School of Economics. Bethany had since moved into the private sector where she was a renowned expert on alternative currencies and investment vehicles. With a single search, they surfaced a half dozen articles on her most recent pet project: nonfungible tokens and their investment utility.

"Explains why Catherine was comfortable strolling in public with her," Levi said. "Bethany is a public figure already."

"And Catherine's new favorite launderer?" Julia speculated.

"Probably not her per se," Marsh said. "But the vehicle, yes. NFTs are the new darling of launderers. No regulation makes it easier than even bitcoin."

"Either way," Sean said, "the meeting doesn't raise eyebrows. It looks like Catherine visiting a trusted friend to do her banker due diligence. Any investment firm has to be looking into NFTs right now."

One connection and motive sorted, they moved on to the couple in Karlsruhe. They were not as readily identified because, as it turned out, they had no connections to the town or Germany. Jessica and Evan Hagan were American tourists passing through Karlsruhe on the train. Whether their meeting was happenstance or planned, Marsh's team would never know, but it had been productive for Catherine. And for them. With the few words Levi had picked up, Marsh had cross-checked Eder Capital's contact management system he'd hacked against US transportation companies, then narrowed that list by filtering for donors of Representative Anthony's opponents. That produced a much smaller list from which Sean had identified the Hagans with his own industry knowledge.

Levi identified the motive. "Trafficking routes."

"Interestingly," Binny said, "the Hagans are contacts of Charles's. The professor and our stranger from the train"— he flipped his computer around—"Ash Sinclair, a person with known ties to the same ISIS cell as Bauer, are contacts of Catherine's."

"Hold that thought," Levi said to Binny with a raised finger, then asked Marsh, "Did you check the group downstairs already?"

Marsh nodded. "Tapped into hotel surveillance, got pictures of each, and ran them through facial recognition. Most are Catherine's colleagues at the investment firm. Two are neighbors. None have criminal records or criminal associates, other than Catherine, and I doubt any of them know she is a criminal."

"That squares," Levi said. "Catherine told me they were her friends. I tend to believe her. She was a different person with them."

Marsh trusted his husband's judgment. Levi had read Catherine Sanders pretty well even before he'd spent the past twenty-four hours watching her work. Marsh circled back to the other open item instead. "You picked up something else today?" he asked Levi. "About what she was doing?"

Levi crossed a leg Marsh's direction and slumped sideways in his chair, shoulder against the padded back. For a split second, it felt like being back home at the start of all this, him and Levi decorating the walls of the upstairs office while they traded theories and built their case. But then one of the planes from Heathrow rumbled overhead, and it sounded nothing like the fighter jets that rumbled over the house in San Diego.

Levi tapped his calf with his toe, drawing Marsh back to the present. "You with me?"

"I was at home in San Diego."

"Soon, fellas," Julia said. "We're still on this side of the pond for now. What else did you learn today, Levi?"

He left his foot tucked under Marsh's leg, keeping them connected, as he explained his latest theory on the case. "I started the day thinking Catherine was trying to steal her uncle's trafficking routes, then I thought maybe she was trying to prove herself the rightful heir so he'd give them to her, but that's not her Plan A."

"She's building her own empire," Marsh deduced, and Levi nodded.

"So she's not out to steal EC from her uncle?" Sean asked.

"Oh, I think she would in a heartbeat," Levi said. "And she's got a window of opportunity to do so while the spotlight is on Charles and Anthony, but that would just be gravy."

"But she's on her way to jail," Julia said. "She gets that, right?"

"Since when has that stopped a criminal?" Binny mused aloud.

Levi chuckled. "That's exactly what she said."

Binny shifted his computer to the side and propped his elbows on the table. "The Hagans are her US transport routes." He lifted one finger. "The professor gave her insights, possibly contacts, for laundering funds via NFTs." Raised a second finger. "Ash is the European end of the supply chain." Three fingers. "She'll need one in the US if she doesn't already have it."

And that's where Marsh and Levi had her. From the word go. "Phase three," Marsh said, referring to the EC paths he and Levi had first outlined in San Diego.

Levi grinned, confirming he'd followed correctly. "She has to solicit new clients."

"She tried deterrence and retribution." Marsh explained their thinking to the others. "Neither of those worked. We have EC on their heels. Catherine has to look outside the usual circle."

"For clients she can keep for herself," Binny said, catching on, then throwing a curveball. "Or present to her uncle if she decides that's the smarter play."

"Has to be considered," Marsh conceded. "Either way, we lead her to clients who are in our pocket."

"Ross and Wagner can get us a list of Stefan's supply chain contacts in the US."

"I'm not sure how much of that he controlled," Marsh said, remembering his words from the interrogation.

"If there are any," Levi said, "we'll need to confirm those contacts are Stefan's and not EC's."

"And besides," Marsh said, "we might have a cleaner option." He and Levi had discussed it as one of their many contingencies. They hadn't exercised it yet because they hadn't wanted to put more of their friends and family at risk, but Marsh trusted their contacts a hell of a lot more than any Stefan might provide. "How soon can we get flight clearance out of here?" he asked Sean.

Levi shot out a hand and clutched his thigh. Hard. "You're leaving?"

"The sooner I get to San Francisco, the sooner we both get home to San Diego."

"You don't even know if she's there."

Marsh covered his hand and coaxed Levi to flip his grip. He laced their fingers together and gently squeezed. "Brax and Mel will get her there by the time I arrive, and everything will be ready by the time you and Catherine land." He glanced again at Sean. "How soon?"

Sean checked the time on his phone. "It's a busy airport, but at this time of night, it's mostly mail and package couriers. We've got a couple hours before passenger traffic picks back up."

"Make it three," he said, banking a little more time for him and Levi. "And let's get Charlie and her SAC on the phone. We're going to need Conder to work some more of his magic." The right spell, the right trap, and hopefully they'd all be home soon.

NINE

BY THE TIME flight plans had been changed, tickets rebooked, and clearances obtained, there was less than an hour left before Marsh was scheduled to depart with Sean and Julia. As much as Levi hated it, he understood why Marsh had to arrive in advance. If they were going to convince Catherine, Marsh would have to carefully work his connections to lay the groundwork, and Levi would have to sell the shit out of it to Catherine. Levi trusted Marsh to deliver, and Marsh was trusting him to do the same, was trusting him to execute the final phase of the plan they'd put in place over a month ago. Starting with a marriage proposal Levi, at the time, had thought absurd. He brushed his thumb over his wedding band, his soul at peace now that the ring was back where it belonged. Further proof his and Marsh's marriage was far from absurd. Was more real than ever. The man beside him at the table, sexy as hell in his glasses and rumpled from the long hours of work, was the person Levi wanted to spend the rest of his life with. Wanted to spend the next hour with for certain.

Alone.

"Are we all set?" Levi asked once Binny wrapped his call with Sutton. When everyone around the table nodded, he pushed back and stood. "All right, then. I'd like to spend what little time I have left with my husband."

In a rare show of acquiescence—or more likely, the truth of how tired everyone really was—there were zero complaints to adjourning. Not even from Binny. He called down to Sal to confirm Catherine's whereabouts, then trudged out the door. Sean and Julia followed after a last check of departure times.

Leaving Levi and Marsh alone. Finally.

Marsh closed his laptop and tossed his glasses on top of it. He scrubbed his hands over his face and groaned behind his fingers. "You can't say things like that."

Levi scooted in front of Marsh, knocking his knees wide enough to stand between the vee of his thighs. "Like what?" he asked coyly. He carded his fingers through Marsh's dark hair and waited for the purr of appreciation. He didn't get it. Instead, Marsh lowered his hands and tipped up his chin. His expression was as close to pained as Levi had seen it since their flight from San Diego to Texas. "Baby, what is it?"

Marsh lightly clasped his waist and gave him a gentle jostle. "Don't say things like 'what little time I have left.'"

Oh.

Levi closed the distance between them, folding Marsh into his embrace and tucking his head beneath his chin. "I just meant here in this hotel room."

"I know." Marsh wound his arms around Levi's waist

and nuzzled into his chest. "But anything could have happened the past twenty-four hours. Any of those people she met could have killed you. She could have killed you. You could have died if Charles had tried to kill her. You—"

"Hey, hey, hey." Levi's heart hurt for Marsh, but it also quietly sang at how endearingly reminiscent Marsh's worst-case ramble was to David's frequent spirals. Less so nowadays, thanks to the man in Levi's arms. He dropped a kiss on the crown of Marsh's head and breathed in the familiar tea tree oil and leather scents. "I'm right here."

"Anything could happen in the *next* twenty-four hours."

Marsh was swinging from the past to the future, fluctuating between the terrible things that might've been and the unknowns that lay ahead. Levi needed Marsh in the present with him. For the good they could have for the next sixty minutes or so. He drew back far enough to cup Marsh's cheeks and tilt his face up. His dark eyes were tortured, same as they'd been that day they'd run from San Diego to Texas, when Marsh had been beating himself up with guilt over the bomb that hadn't been. Levi needed to get him out of that dark place and keep him from going back there ever again. He stepped far enough back to move his legs outside of Marsh's and lower himself onto his lap, crowding him so Levi was all Marsh could see.

"I don't care about the last twenty-four hours or the next twenty-four," Levi said. "Not right now. For the next hour, all I care about is making love to my husband."

Marsh's breath hitched, heat flickered in his eyes, and Levi leaned forward to stoke the fire, to give Marsh the kiss they'd both been wanting since Levi had stepped across that threshold. He wove his fingers through Marsh's hair, holding his head and angling his mouth so Levi could take long, slow sweeps through with his tongue, deep and claiming. Thorough. The way Levi wanted Marsh to take him apart in the time they had left. "Take me to bed, cowboy."

Marsh skated his lips over Levi's jaw and down the column of his throat. "What if I want to take you right here?"

There was his husband. Levi grinned as he arched his neck, giving him better access. "You can take me anywhere." His grin turned to a gasp when Marsh surged out of his chair and tipped him back, Levi's spine meeting the table before he could barely blink.

Dark eyes stared down at him, the guilt gone, no room for it with the desire swirling in Marsh's blown-wide pupils. He planted one hand on the table and used the other to shove his laptop and glasses clear. "We'll start here, then we'll finish in the bedroom."

"I'm good with that."

He was even better with Marsh stripping off his shirt, miles of bronze skin on display, as he stretched back over Levi. He removed Levi's dress shirt one button at a time, peppering each exposed inch of skin with kisses and nips. He lashed a nipple with his tongue, and Levi arched his back, chasing after the teasing heat.

Marsh chuckled, warm breath puffing over Levi's sternum as he kissed across his chest to the other nipple. "You still good?"

Levi plowed a hand into his hair and directed his mouth to its intended target. Marsh seemed to like his answer, working Levi's nipple to just this side of painful. His fingers dug into Levi's thighs, hitching his legs higher over his hips, hauling him closer. He rocked his hips, erection rutting against Levi's. "Holy fuck."

Marsh grinned up at him, lips wet and rosy, more tempting than they had any right to be. "You still good?"

"If by good you mean about to come in my pants, then yeah, baby, I'm fucking spectacular."

"Well, we can't have that." He stepped back, dragging Levi closer to the edge of the table.

Levi moved to loosen and lower his legs. "Thank fu—"

Then swallowed his words, Marsh's left hand closing around his balls. "Can't have you wasting all this goodness in your pants when I'd rather have it in my mouth." Levi cursed a blue streak that made his husband laugh out loud. "Poor baby."

Levi's answering laugh came out a groan. "You better hurry." Which Marsh thankfully did, divesting Levi of his pants and boxers in one go, then swallowing Levi's cock the next. Levi slapped a hand against the table, fingers scrunching pieces of paper in the absence of bedsheets. "Jesus, Marsh." He started to arch again, but Marsh splayed a hand on his abs, keeping Levi pinned to the table, concentrating all his pleasure on his dick that Marsh continued to work hard and rough with his mouth. He didn't go any easier on Levi's other sensitive parts, fondling his balls with zero mercy, aggressively rubbing his taint, rubbing his fingers against his quivering hole, denying him the penetration he craved. None of it was gentle, and all of it was perfect, exactly the way Levi needed it. His husband gave him that, gave him everything he could have wanted and more. Levi exploded. He jack-knifed up, hand fisting Marsh's hair and holding tight as wave after wave of pleasure crested through him. Out of him. Marsh wringing every last drop of come from his dick.

When he was sure there was nothing left, Levi used the hand in Marsh's hair to gently tug him off his spent cock. Hungry eyes clashed with his, and Marsh's erection strained the zipper of his jeans. The best sort of compliment, almost as good as Marsh wiping his mouth with the back of his hand like he'd just finished his favorite meal. Levi's turn to feast, then. He cupped Marsh's shaft through the denim. "I need your cock inside my ass. Now."

Marsh's voice was soaked in lust and gravel. "Is there lube in your bag?" Levi nodded. He hadn't taken it out in the mad dash to pack yesterday morning. "Good," Marsh said as he unbuckled his belt and lowered his zipper. "'Cause I don't think we're gonna make it to the bedroom."

"Good with that too." And with watching Marsh swagger across the room, jeans barely hanging on to his hips. Effortlessly sexy. Levi's cock got interested again, always interested in Marsh, and Levi got moving. He slid off the table, shucked his shirt, and turned. He spread his legs, bent at the waist, and braced a forearm on the table, ass thrust out. He reached his other hand down and stroked himself, moaning softly as he grew hard again.

Marsh moved behind him, drawing Levi's gaze over his shoulder. His cheeks were flushed, his big, beautiful chest heaving, his eyes locked on Levi's hole. He ditched his jeans and boxers, kicked them aside, then tossed the lube onto the table. He stepped close and splayed his hot hands across Levi's ass cheeks, knocking Levi's own hand aside so he could nestle his cock against Levi's taint. "Fuck." The reverence in his groan made Levi want to preen. He rutted back against Marsh's erection as Marsh stretched over him, claiming his lips in a repeat of the deep, plundering kiss Levi had given him earlier. He drew back when they were breathless, when their rocking hips demanded more. "Hold yourself open for me while I finish getting you ready."

Levi groaned, the thought alone ramping him higher. He followed the order, reaching behind himself with both hands and spreading his cheeks. He hissed as his bare chest hit the cool wood and sighed as Marsh's fingers spread lube over and into his hole.

"More," Levi panted and begged. "Please."

Marsh circled his rim, then pushed one finger inside. "Do you know what else you deserve?"

"What?" Levi keened, forehead pressed to the table, ass thrusting back for more. "Tell me."

Marsh kept him in suspense, working him open with a second finger. Levi's arms and hands ached, his dick dripped on the floor, but he didn't let go. Marsh pumped a third finger inside and stretched over him, finally whispering the filthy answer in Levi's ear. "My dick pounding your ass so hard you'll spend all eleven hours of that flight later today thinking of me."

"I'd do that anyway." He craned his neck to look back. He opened his eyes and met his favorite pair over his shoulder. "But yeah, baby, give me that reminder."

Marsh dropped a kiss on his shoulder, so soft, same as his words. "I'll give you everything, Levi. Everything."

Tears pricked the corners of Levi's eyes, but only for a moment until Marsh slammed into him and Levi slammed his eyes shut. The force of Marsh's thrusts took his breath away. Levi loved it, same as he loved the man, same as he loved surrendering everything, his body and soul, to his husband.

"That's it, Levi." Marsh curled over him. "Take it. Take all of me." He peppered his shoulders and spine with more soft kisses. Pounded his ass with his dick, the pace and force relentless. A perfect, devastating combination that made Levi lose his mind, made him beg Marsh to let him come. And when Marsh finally reached a hand around to stroke his cock, when he confessed how badly he'd wanted to do this to Levi that first night they'd fooled around at home, when he pumped his come into Levi with a groan and shout, a promise to do this again when they were home together, Levi soared.

TEN

MARSH HATED San Francisco in the summer. Drippy and fifty in the middle of July was not his idea of a good time. Brax, on the other hand, looked like he was having the time of his life. He stood on the tarmac outside a private-jet hangar, his gaze and bearing calm, the lines of his craggy face smooth, a picture of serenity.

"Still don't get it," Marsh said as he descended the steps of the Paxton plane. He waved his Stetson through the soupy air, collecting cool moisture on the brim. "This is gross and very not summer."

"Better than Texas summer, and the fog will burn off by noon."

"For an hour." Marsh dropped his bags and stepped into his best friend's open arms. "It's good to see you."

Brax hugged him tight, a double back slap before he withdrew and waved to Julia at the door to Sean's plane. "Eagle, thanks for giving him a lift."

"I'll pass it on to Sean," she said. "And for the record, I agree with the nerd on this one."

Marsh flipped his Stetson onto his head. "Two points for real summer."

"And on that note," Julia said, "I'm headed someplace sunny."

"Traitor!" Marsh called her direction. They were all better rested and a measure lighter this morning. They were back on their side of the pond, Levi only a few hours behind them, and with a solid game plan moving forward, assuming Marsh could pull this meet off without a hitch.

"Get your work done, Agent Marshall," Julia said as the mechanical steps lifted. "Then get your ass home. I expect you in the office this week."

Home. He liked the sound of that. Sun, San Diego, a job and colleagues he enjoyed, a husband and son he couldn't wait to spend the rest of his life with. Foggy San Francisco was a pit stop on the way there—and someplace they'd have to visit frequently for family, just not in the summer.

"Reinstated?" Brax asked as he picked up one of Marsh's bags and turned toward the hangar.

Marsh grabbed the other and followed. "For now."

"Hopefully, the operation here won't compromise that."

"We ran it through Charlie and Sutton Conder in DC. He signed off for organized crime, Binny for legat, Cam for the applicable field offices. It's all sanctioned."

"Relatively," came a familiar voice from the hangar's second floor. Melissa Cruz stood braced against the metal catwalk that ran the length of one side of the space, maintenance bays below for the private jet to their right, a couple of bare bones offices, a conference room, and a bunk room above for when Redemption Inc., the bounty hunter business she ran with Brax, needed them.

Marsh removed his hat. "Cruz, good to see you again."

The former Special Agent in Charge leaned her toned forearms against the metal rail and stared down at him with dark, devilish eyes. "Sounds like I'm also adding you to the official trouble-maker list."

"If he"—Marsh tipped his hat toward Brax—"didn't warn you of that already, he's a shit business partner."

Brax dropped the heavy bag on Marsh's foot. "Fuck you."

Laughing, Marsh glanced between the two of them. "Thanks for setting this up."

"Group effort." She straightened and waved them up. "Leave your bags. We'll get them on the way out."

Marsh rescued his foot from under the one bag, dropped the one he was carrying beside it, then followed Brax up the stairs. "How's David?"

"Under Holt's watch," Brax confirmed. "He's an amazing kid."

"I know. Not sure how I got so lucky, but I know."

They crested the stairs, and Brax clasped his shoulder. "I'm happy for you."

"Good," he said as they traveled the catwalk to the conference room. "Hopefully, you won't mind spending your wedding anniversary in San Diego this year." Brax cocked a brow, and Marsh spun the ring around his finger, failing to hide his grin. "We kind of promised David and my moms a wedding. One they get to attend this time."

Brax matched his smile and dragged him into a sideways hug. "We wouldn't miss it."

"Am I invited too?" Helena Madigan asked. Holt's sister and the second most dangerous woman Marsh had ever met, behind only Mel, waited for them at the door to the conference room. Long blond curls bouncing, she turned up her cheek like her niece so often did.

Marsh leaned forward and kissed it. "Of course, gorgeous."

"This whole reunion thing is cute," a sharp, lightly accented Russian voice said. "But the clock's ticking."

Marsh had seen photos of Remy Pak before but pictures didn't always translate presence. And Remy had it. Dressed in dark jeans, a fitted leather jacket, and knee-high combat boots, the striking woman with cool undertones beneath her light tan skin, her dark hair gathered in a high, tight bun, was the human personification of the deadly weapons she ran for the Russian mob. She'd pinged federal law enforcement's radar years ago, only now she was a double agent, brought in by Hawes Madigan's husband, a former ATF agent. She was also a Madigan frenemy and a reluctant Redemption asset. Her reputation preceded her.

"Agent Marshall," Mel said, "Remy Pak. Remy, this is Marsh."

He'd normally smirk and make a flirty remark, flexing his charm to see how it would be received, but some instinct told Marsh his balls were safer behind manners where Remy was concerned. He removed his hat and held out a hand. "Ma'am. Thank you for meeting with us."

She shook his hand, then rested back against the table's edge near Helena. "You have access to a channel my boss would like to reopen."

That didn't make sense. He cut a questioning glance Mel and Brax's direction.

"My other boss," Remy clarified.

Oh.

Maybe Marsh needed more sleep since her meaning

hadn't clicked the first time. Maybe they needed to reconsider this plan altogether. He tossed his hat onto the table and crossed his arms, fingers digging into his biceps. "I'm not interested in putting more guns or people in the Bratva's hands. I just need Catherine Sanders to think that's what she's doing long enough to arrest her."

"Potato, potahto." Remy shrugged. "I'll help you with this. What happens after…"

Helena stepped between them, squaring off with Remy. "I'll call Agent Salty on your ass."

She rolled her eyes and flicked a dismissive hand. "Fuck off, bitch."

"Children," Mel chided with a poorly concealed smirk.

Tension cut, Marsh chuckled and stepped closer to Brax, lowering his voice. "How's life as a babysitter?"

Brax's answering grin was bright enough to burn off the fog outside. "Fucking spectacular."

"I'm happy for you too," Marsh said genuinely beyond thrilled his best friend got a second chance at the love of his life and a second—third—career that suited him so well.

"All right, then." Mel moved to the head of the table and gestured for everyone to take a seat. "Let's figure out what we can and need to document so I can get Agents Byrne and Henby what they need."

Marsh claimed the chair beside Brax, Helena and Remy the ones across from them. "You can't be at the meet," Remy said to him as she flung his Stetson back across the table. "You scream fed."

"That's a first." Marsh couldn't recall anyone ever saying he actually looked the part.

Brax bumped a shoulder against his. "Your husband might make an honest man out of you yet."

"He as obvious as you?" Remy asked.

"He can pull it off," Marsh assured her.

The discussion turned to logistics after that—the where and when of a meet between Catherine and Remy, who would facilitate, what they needed Catherine to say and do, and where and when Remy was supposed to end things. Marsh still wasn't convinced she actually would, but finalizing a plan that put Catherine Sanders behind bars, that would lead to Charles Sanders and Stewart Anthony there too, and that ended Eder Capital and a racist bigot's presidential hopes would ultimately balance out any damage Remy could do.

They were just finishing when Marsh's phone rang, Julia's name lighting up the screen. "You at cruising altitude already?"

"Negative," she replied. "Just touched back down in San Francisco."

He stood, exited the conference room, and peered out the hangar doors. No accident that he could see; no Paxton plane in sight yet either. "What's going on?"

"We're coming back to get you. You're needed in San Diego. Now."

"But I'm needed here." Levi would land in a few hours, Marsh would run comms on the op they'd spent the last half hour planning, and then both of them would be on their way home. Together. This would all be over.

"We found Greg and Amanda Hudson. Dead."

Or things were further from over than ever.

ELEVEN

THE FLIGHT from San Francisco to Carlsbad took less time than the relatively short but traffic-packed drive from the airport to Temecula. The same airport Marsh had flown out of three weeks ago. Three weeks and a lifetime. That had been one of the worst days of Marsh's life, when the future he had only just begun to believe was possible had almost slipped through his fingers. Was almost stolen by murderers he and Levi had spent the past three weeks chasing. And now they'd murdered again by the look of it. Several Bureau sedans, a crime scene unit van, and a Riverside County coroner's vehicle were parked in front of the end unit of a single-story industrial building, one of four Marsh counted in the freeway-adjacent complex.

"Only the coroner from local?" he asked.

"And the deputy sheriff," Julia said as she parked in an open spot across the lot. "He's a transplant from LA. Someone Matt knew and sweet talked into keeping this quiet for a few hours. But this close to the freeway"—she jutted her chin at the I-15 on the other side of the complex's chain link fence—"it's only a matter of time before someone from the local PD drives by and wonders why there's no chatter about this on the radio."

"We better move, then." Marsh reached between the seats, grabbed his hat out of the back, then shoved open the car door. He got as far as closing it behind him when his phone pinged. He pulled it out of his pocket and opened the text from Sean.

Anthony press conference tomorrow afternoon. Announcing exploratory committee.

He held the text open on-screen long enough for Julia to read. She glanced up from the phone, over to the crime scene, then back to him. "We might have some counterprogramming here."

He pocketed the phone and started across the parking lot beside her. "That's exactly what I'm thinking, depending on what we find."

A linebacker of a white man with dark hair and dark eyes appeared on the other side of the coroner's van. "Agents!" he called, flagging them down. Even if Marsh hadn't already met Agent Byrne in San Francisco or recognized his Southie accent, the Celtics tee he proudly wore would've been a dead giveaway. "Cam," Marsh greeted, hand extended. "You planning to be the next murder victim, wearing that shirt in Lakers country?"

He laughed as he shook Marsh's hand. "A little purple and gold don't scare me." He shook Julia's hand next. "Agent Kwan, welcome back. Apologies for not leaving you a day off before jumping back in."

"What's a day off?" Julia replied, and they all shared a laugh as they started toward the unit bustling with agents and crime scene techs. "I'm sure this isn't the way you prefer missing persons cases to go either."

"Never the end we want," Cam said, "but not unexpected this time."

"Did they come through the bay here?" Marsh asked as they passed under the roll-up door.

Cam pointed at the in-wall door to their right. "Entered through that door."

"Any signs of forced entry?" Julia asked.

"None," Alyssa answered as she left one group, including Farmer and Will, outside an interior door on the left side of the space to join theirs. "They either had the key or someone was a half-decent lock pick."

"Older lock," Cam added. "Not that hard."

Marsh lifted a brow. "Got some experience, Agent Byrne?"

"I wasn't always a happily wedded fed."

"They were holed up here?" Julia asked. "The entire time?"

"We think so," Alyssa answered. She pointed at what looked like a cordoned off kitchenette to the left of the room where most of the crime scene activity was focused. "There's stuff in the fridge on the fringe."

"The amount of luggage and detritus also point to a long-term stay," Cam added.

Marsh glanced around the rest of the space. Work benches lined the entire back wall, greasy tools and random car parts on top and in bins below, and a rusted-out car body sat under a pulled back tarp in the back right corner. "Who owns the space? A mechanic?"

Cam nodded toward the office directly to their right. Inside, Matt and a Black man with a sheriff's badge on his lapel sat across a desk from a gray-haired white woman Marsh would guess was somewhere in her seventies. "Her husband used to restore cars here."

"Used to?"

"He passed a few months ago."

Julia cursed. "And now this?"

"Not her best year," Alyssa concurred. "She stayed at the shelter an age ago when she was getting back on her feet after an abusive relationship. She's still a donor."

"Amanda saw the obituary," Cam continued. "She approached the owner about using the space for temporary shelter storage."

One last con while they figured out how to flee. Where had their plan gone off the rails? "Kwan said you found them?" Marsh asked.

"Thanks to your guy in protective custody."

"Frederick?" He was the ACH processor Amanda's boyfriend had used to embezzle funds from his employer and launder them through bitcoin. A trick he'd learned from Amanda, who, with her father, worked with Frederick to do the same for Orchard Investments, Eder Capital's West Coast front.

Cam nodded. "He had a list of all the Orchard bitcoin accounts."

"Amanda accessed one?" She'd know the risk; they must have been desperate.

"Tried to," Farmer said as he joined them. The cyber agent's ears must have been burning. "She created a new account, tried to make a deposit into one of their older, dormant accounts, and hit a wall since we froze all the Orchard ones. We picked up the ping, then followed where she went. She sent a payment out to another account for 'services rendered.'"

"She was going to launder it through Orchard," Marsh pieced together aloud.

"For what?" Julia asked.

"To pay Blaine Anthony," Alyssa answered. "For two fake IDs."

Fucking hell. "How long ago?"

"Friday," Farmer answered.

Julia's gaze snapped to Marsh. "She and her father got word of the benefit in Salzburg, what happened with Catherine, Charles, and Anthony."

Marsh nodded. "Last chance to run. Anthony would clean up anything that threatened his candidacy."

Alyssa wondered aloud what they were all thinking. "Including his son?"

Couldn't be dismissed, but Marsh didn't think—hoped —it wasn't Anthony's first instinct.

"Amanda had to know she was taking a risk," Julia said, "contacting Anthony's son for help."

"But she trusted him enough," Marsh said. "Might be something we can use."

Julia turned her attention to Farmer. "How'd you use that to locate them here?"

"IP address. She used a computer at a nearby public library."

"From there we pulled surveillance from any camera in the vicinity," Cam said.

"So many hours of footage," Alyssa groaned.

"But you found it." Cam chuckled. "A delivery person dropped groceries outside this unit last week."

"And between then and now…" Julia prompted.

Cam led them to the bunk room at the back of the unit. He, Alyssa, and Farmer hung back while Marsh followed Julia inside the room, careful to stay in the designated areas and not to disturb any evidence. The coroner was working over a body bag on the floor. Amanda. There was another zipped bag behind the coroner, Greg, Marsh assumed. Aside from the lingering scent of bodily fluids recently discharged, there was no smell of decay, and Amanda's skin wasn't slack or gray yet. "This is recent?" Marsh asked.

The coroner glanced over her shoulder. "Within the last twenty-four hours."

"Any sign of a struggle?" He didn't guess so given the bullet wound to Amanda's forehead, but he couldn't see her hands from where he was standing.

"Shot in their sleep." The coroner moved back enough for Marsh to see the second gunshot wound to Amanda's chest. "Execution style. I've seen enough gang hits out this way to know."

"This was a hit," Julia said as they rejoined the others.

"Sure looks like it," Marsh concurred just as the office door opened across the bay.

Matt exited alone, the deputy sheriff remaining in the office with the owner.

Which gave Marsh the opening to lighten the mood they all needed. "Should you even be out in the field?"

Matt answered as Marsh expected. "Fuck you very much."

The laughter was welcome, Matt's hug even more so. "Aww, Agent Kim, did you miss me?"

"You and your better half."

He drew back, arm over Matt's shoulders. "He'll be here before long."

Cam grinned. "It's good to see you making new friends, Matty K."

Matt scowled and shook a finger at his old partner. "Don't you start."

More laughter. Until Julia brought them back to the depressing earth. "Anything else useful from the owner?"

He shook his head. "Just some finer details on the when of communications with Amanda. But it all tracks with what she told us before. She doesn't recall telling anyone they were here."

"Has she visited at all since they've been here?"

"No, she hasn't been back since the day she met them here with the keys."

"So just the delivery person," Marsh said.

"Only one time," Alyssa added.

"And the fake IDs?" Julia asked.

"Haven't found them yet."

"Any activity on their bank or credit cards?" Marsh asked.

"None," Farmer confirmed.

"On their cards," Matt said. "Let's also run a check if there were any stolen cards reported in the area."

"And double-check with shelter staff," Marsh suggested. "They may not have noticed until recently."

Farmer and Alyssa stepped away, drawing Will into their huddle as they began running down the requested information.

Marsh, meanwhile, glanced back over his shoulder, trying to piece together exactly what had happened here the past twenty-four hours. "How did the killer find them? And why not get rid of the bodies?"

"We're working on the first," Cam said. "Trying to find the delivery person and Blaine Anthony."

"As for the second," Matt said, "we can only speculate at this point. Most obvious is that the killer thought they wouldn't be found until decomposition had set in."

"Or maybe they got interrupted," Cam said. "By Blaine Anthony or someone delivering those IDs."

Marsh threw out another possibility. "Or the killer was just that arrogant. Fits the Eder MO."

Julia nodded at his side. "You thinking what I'm thinking, Nerd?"

"That it's always the little things"—like arrogance—"that trip up the biggest criminals."

TWELVE

"ARE you going to tell me now why we used fake passports to board a flight to San Francisco instead of DC?" Catherine shivered as she dug through her luggage for a sweater. The linen jumpsuit she'd worn for travel comfort and for what she'd anticipated would be a summer day in DC was no match for July on the fog-shrouded San Francisco Bay. "And whose yacht are we on?"

A heeled leather boot appeared at the top of the upper-deck ladder. "I can answer the second question," the woman in denim and leather said as she descended the stairs. "But first I need to sweep you for bugs."

Levi recognized Remy Pak from her faint Russian accent and from the photos Marsh had briefed him on, but even without the pictures, even without the accent, her bearing, once she stood on the stern deck with them, was unmistakable. She carried herself with the kind of fuck-off energy that made even Catherine take a step back.

Remy retrieved a wand from under one of the bench seats, swiped it over him and Catherine and their bags, then tossed the wand back under the seat. "The yacht belongs to my boss," she said. "Dimitri Petrov."

Catherine's eyes widened. "Which makes you Remy Pak."

"Good. You know why I'm here, then."

"I can assume." Wrapped in Burberry, the fake Londoner seemed better suited to the fog. Or maybe it was just her shield back up, Catherine's back straight and balance found now that the initial shock of the meet had passed. "I hope it's the same reason I am."

"I heard"—Remy glanced at Levi, then back to Catherine—"that you were looking for new channels of business. Whether it's for yourself or your uncle, my boss would be interested in hearing more. Our relationship with Eder Capital in the past was mutually beneficial."

"Can we have a moment?" Catherine said to Remy, then hand on Levi's arm, walked him a few steps out of Remy's earshot. "You're setting me up," she whispered through clenched teeth.

"No," Levi replied. "I'm setting myself up. Financially. Our reinstatements were revoked." Or so went the cover story Levi's team had put in place in the wee hours of the London morning. "Which is why we had to use the fake passports."

Eyes narrowed, brow pinched, Catherine remained skeptical. "I thought your husband was wealthy."

"He is," Levi admitted. "But I learned the hard way how fast circumstances can change. I will not have the rug pulled out from under my son again." Not a lie. Just the truth reframed in a way that would appeal to Catherine's independent streak and self-interest.

Her scowl was slow to temper—she eyed him for any

sign of a lie—but eventually judging him truthful, a small smile turned up one corner of her mouth. She eased the grip on his arm and patted his shoulder like a proud best friend. "There's that backbone I knew you had in you, Levi."

"We do what we have to do," he said, repeating back his earlier words to her. The other corner of her lips rose, a full-fledged smile, and she turned back to Remy, more of her confidence returned. It faltered only slightly when, after a few steps, she realized Levi hadn't followed. "Go on," he said. "I'm going to call my son."

The scowl flirted again with the hairline wrinkles at the corners of her eyes. "You don't want all the details?"

"Not if I want to sleep at night." And not if he wanted to convince Catherine this wasn't a trap. Which it totally was. He couldn't sit there and listen to her and Remy discuss trafficking weapons and people and not react. Not after years of work locking up criminals like Remy and Catherine for doing exactly that. Turning a blind ear and pretending to be an ostrich was his only play to maintain cover. He prayed Marsh's and the Madigans' trust in Remy to report back whatever arrangements she made with Catherine was not misplaced.

Leaving the two of them on the stern deck, Levi moseyed around to the promenade and leaned against the rail. He squinted, trying to make out the Ferry Building through the fog. Maybe that was the clock tower? Who could navigate anything in this pea soup? He withdrew his phone and opened his encrypted chat with Marsh. **Package delivered.**

Marsh texted back almost immediately. **G. A. H. Dead. Temecula. Stay sharp.**

It took Levi a moment to decipher the message but when he did, he jolted off the rail. He scanned the area around him and the yacht, cursing the fog that hid any threats, the number of them suddenly multiplying in his head. Greg and Amanda Hudson had been found dead in Temecula, halfway between Riverside and San Diego. Not what he wanted to hear when David was supposed to fly home tomorrow. **Is it still safe for D there?**

Will check the house over with the team tonight. It'll be a fortress by the time we're done.

But even a fortress wouldn't have kept out the bomb that almost stole his son's life three weeks ago.

We'll have protection too, Marsh added. **I wouldn't risk him if I didn't think we could keep him safe. If we didn't need him home with us.**

And David needed to be home. He'd said as much to Levi last night. **He needs to be home with us too.**

Brax will be there with the plane first thing tomorrow.

I'll call and tell David.

They signed off with I love yous, then Levi closed the app and dialed David.

"Hey, Dad," he answered after a few rings. "You want me to switch to video?"

Levi wanted nothing more in that moment than to see his son's face, but he couldn't compromise his safety either. "Can't right now, buddy."

Worry shot through David's voice. "Is everything okay? Where are you?"

"I'm in San Francisco."

And vanished, replaced with thinly veiled excitement. "San Francisco? I thought you were going to DC."

"Change of plans. Things are moving faster than we hoped, which is why I'm calling."

"Please say what I think you're going to say." He repeated the phrase twice more, and each time, he somehow made please sound like a three-syllable word.

Levi laughed. Fuck, he loved his kid. On this very long, very gray day, from two time zones away, he managed to brighten Levi's day. Levi was happy to return the favor. "Brax will be there with the plane tomorrow to take you home. That good enough?"

"Fuck yeah!"

"Language," Levi corrected absently, otherwise caught up in imagining David doing a happy dance in the stables. He was probably scaring the poor baby goats.

"Will you be there too?" David asked. "Marsh?"

"Marsh will meet you at the airport in San Diego. I'll be there in a couple days."

"Yee-haw!" Make that a two-step happy dance, complete with cowboy hat.

Levi leaned back against the rail, grinning. "What's the neighborhood going to do with the Texa-fied version of you?"

"Not just me." David laughed. "Me and Marsh."

"Fucking hell," Levi muttered.

"Language!" David threw back at him.

More sunshine wrapped around Levi, buffering him against the fog, buoying him after days, weeks, years of hard times for both of them. "I'm proud of you, David. I know this hasn't been easy, but seeing you thrive, even under the pressure of the past several weeks, it's what me and your mom always wanted, always knew you were capable of."

David quieted, and Levi worried maybe he'd said the wrong thing by bringing up Kristin. But when his son spoke again, his voice was still bright, contemplative, not sad. "I think maybe I need some pressure. Not like you and Marsh level pressure. I could never do the law enforcement or military thing. Not my deal. More like Irina level pressure with the vet thing. Is that still on the table?"

"Being a vet is pressure-filled too," Levi cautioned. "It's not all cute baby goats."

"I know," he said, tone serious. "Irina's been sure to tell me about the schooling and the practice and about losing patients too. I'm not one hundred percent sold, but I want to look into it. Maybe find an internship that's not working for Aunt Nic."

"Hmm," Levi said, drawing out his hum into as many syllables as David had his earlier please. "Sounds more like a you not working for Aunt Nic thing versus a you working for a vet thing."

"Bit of both," his son admitted. "Not gonna lie."

They both laughed, and Levi encouraged David to tell him more about his day-to-day as a vet's assistant. He listened with rapt attention until the pop of a champagne cork clued him in to Catherine and Remy's meeting wrapping up. Successfully, it seemed. He straightened from the rail and glanced over his shoulder in time to see Catherine appear at the end of the promenade, two raised glasses in hand.

He raised his hand for her to wait. "All right, buddy, this has been great, but I gotta go." He slowly walked Catherine's direction as he finished with David. "Be good for Marsh, and I'll see you soon."

"Will do, love you, Dad."

"Love you too." He ended the call just as he reached the end of the promenade.

"Everything good?" Catherine asked as she held a glass out to him.

"My son wants to be a vet."

"Well, when we're done here, you'll have plenty of money to send him to whatever vet school he wants." She tapped the rim of her glass against his. "Cheers, Mr. Bishop."

Cheers, indeed, to setting phase three officially in motion and to getting home to his family sooner rather than later.

THIRTEEN

THE BAY BRIDGE was in sight, the arena and ballpark even closer, but before reaching either, the yacht's captain turned the boat down one of the many commercial canals that flowed between the industrial piers. He slowed behind the U-shaped building with Madigan Cold Storage emblazoned on the eyebrow, smoothly steering the yacht into the smaller of the two berths, the one with a suited Hawes Madigan waiting by the mooring post.

"Remy," he greeted, the coolness in his tone—the opposite of hospitality—almost enough to make Levi laugh.

Remy did cackle like she was used to Hawes's chill and enjoyed working him up. She tossed him the mooring rope. "Where's your sister?"

"At home with her wife and kids," Hawes said as he looped the rope around the post.

They worked together to unfold the gangway, and Remy continued to needle him, clicking her tongue against her teeth. "That's a shame." When she didn't get the rise she wanted out of him, she returned her attention to Catherine. "I'll be in touch. It won't be long."

"I'll have everything in place when you call," Catherine said with a pleased smile. She cinched the belt of her coat and grabbed her roller bag. "It's been a pleasure, Ms. Pak."

Levi gave their temporary host a parting nod, then followed Catherine off the boat. They stood to the side as Hawes and Remy folded up the gangway and unmoored the boat, no more words between them, clearly more enemies than friends. Once the yacht was on its way, Hawes turned his icy gaze on Catherine. "Hawes Madigan," he introduced himself, voice and manner impossibly colder. Not a greeting at all.

"Catherine Sanders." She kept her own hands shoved in her pockets. "I understand you're responsible for the death of two mercenaries I hired in Texas."

Bile rocketed up Levi's throat, and the dizziness he'd felt at the benefit in Salzburg the other night walloped him again. Catherine had told him then that she'd sent hired guns after his son and husband's family. He'd believed her, but actually hearing her confirm what she'd done… The only thing that kept Levi upright now was the parallel confirmation that the Madigans had protected them, that they truly did have Levi's family's back.

"You hired the wrong mercenaries," Hawes told Catherine, and Levi couldn't recall ever hearing someone talk so coolly to her. A blow after her other "wins" today.

Playing coy, she leaned into Levi and tried to yank him back into the conversation. "My, my, Mr. Bishop, you do keep some interesting company."

Levi hadn't missed how she'd dropped the "agent" since he'd told her his reinstatement had been revoked. He hitched his bag between them, creating space and refusing to buffer her against Hawes's chill. "If you did any background checks at all, you knew my husband was best friends with Braxton Kane, who is married to Hawes's twin brother."

"Yes, but Mr. Kane was previously law enforcement. So was Mr. Madigan's husband. I assumed their goal was to turn their husbands and the Madigans straight."

"No one in this family is straight, Ms. Sanders," Hawes deadpanned. "In any sense of the word."

Catherine tilted her head, eyes narrowed. Assessing the person who had seemingly stumped her. She always had an angle, a play, but she clearly didn't know what to make of Hawes Madigan. "I had heard you'd retired." She flicked her gaze to the building behind them. "That you were running your family's cold storage business."

"Yes, I focus my efforts on MCS now. My sister runs our other business, which has become more discerning in its operations. But make no mistake, we are still the best at what we do." He stepped closer and lowered his voice, a menacing edge to it that sent chills up Levi's spine. "And if you come at our family again, which includes Marsh and Levi, their son, and their families, we will end you."

Catherine white-knuckled her suitcase handle at the same time she straightened her spine and lifted her chin, trying to maintain a confident front. "Prince of Killers. Makes sense."

"King now, and Hawes will do just fine." His light blue eyes shifted to Levi, but his words were still directed at Catherine. "Levi and Marsh want to do this the civilized way." His gaze hardened and swung back to Catherine. "I will do it any way I can to protect my family."

He didn't wait for Catherine's reply. Or maybe her sharp inhale was reply enough. He turned up the path to the building, expecting them to follow. Catherine, however, remained frozen to the spot, any color the earlier champagne had given her pale cheeks gone. She was on her heels, all four designer inches of them, and as much as Levi wanted to lean in and whisper *Did you know I had the most dangerous piece on the board?* he kept his mouth shut and gently nudged her forward, his own knees steadier now thanks to the king.

Inside the facility, Levi barely got a look around the ground floor—production and storage as far as he could tell—before they rode the elevator up to the third floor. In silence. Broken only when the doors opened and Levi let out a surprised gasp. Helena Madigan, wearing a black suit compared to her brother's gray, waited for them at the reception desk, not at home with her wife and kids as Hawes had led Remy and them to believe. Catherine was surprised too, her steps stuttering as she preceded Hawes out of the cab.

"Catherine Sanders," Hawes said, "my sister, Helena Madigan. Helena, this is Catherine."

The petite blond Levi had first seen in the airport weeks ago shot him a wink, same as she had then before wiping all trace of warmth from her expression. She pinned Catherine with an icy glare that bested her brother's. "He give you the stay away from our family warning?"

Catherine nodded. "He did."

"If you don't believe him, believe me." In the half second Levi glanced at Catherine to assess her reaction, a knife was hurtled their direction. It sliced through the narrow space between their heads, hissing as it cut through the air on the way to lodging in the wall behind them. Levi whipped his gaze back to Helena, who stood with her arms crossed as if she'd merely flicked a paper football at them, zero effort exerted to so expertly throw that knife. Correction. Helena Madigan was the most dangerous piece on the board, and thank fuck the queen was on his and Marsh's side.

"Understood," Catherine said, a slight tremor in her voice. She cleared her throat and started again. "If you have a few minutes, I'd like to get your read on Remy Pak," she said, seeking firmer, common ground.

Helena laughed out loud, the icy cold mask shattering. "Let's head into my office," she said. "This will take a while." She led them past the reception desk and into a hallway of executive offices, diverting into the first one on the right. Levi moved to follow, but Hawes's hand around his biceps directed him farther down the hallway instead, past an oversized office-slash-command center-slash-play-room, then another more reasonably sized office with stacks of paper on the desk, before reaching the office at the far corner. Hawes closed the door behind them, and the tension he'd been carrying since the dock seeped from his frame. Not ice cracking like his sister; more like ice melting, revealing the friendly if deliberative man Levi had inter-acted with several times on calls and briefly in Texas. He wasn't as warm and open as Holt or Brax, but the evidence of his love and devotion was everywhere around his office from the photo of him and his husband on his desk, the drawings by Lily that decorated his whiteboard, and the collection of family wedding photos that graced his credenza. There was warmth there, just quieter than the other members of his family.

Speaking of quiet... "The offices are soundproof?" Levi asked as he dropped his bag by the door and slid into one of the visitor chairs.

Hawes tossed his suit jacket across the desk. He folded into the visitor chair beside Levi, his smirk completely transforming his face, turning all those hard lines and sharp angles from menacing to devastating. "Comes in handy with three siblings who love their spouses. A lot."

Levi chuckled. "Also with a kid who is around often." He tipped his head to the whiteboard stick figures. "I noticed the setup in the office beside Helena's."

"Holt's," Hawes confirmed. "Or more accurately, Lily's."

"I remember those days. David's toys used to be scattered from one end of the house to the other, upstairs and downstairs." Now all that clutter was concentrated in his lair. Levi marveled at how David had survived this long in Texas with no video game console and only a single suitcase of belongings. Marveled at how well he seemed to be doing. Was it the truth? Or an act so Levi wouldn't worry? "How is he? For real? He sounds and looks good on calls, but not being there, it's hard to tell."

Hawes reached out and covered Levi's hand, the warmth surprising. "He's good, Levi. He's an incredible kid." He gave his hand a squeeze then drew back into his chair. "And I meant what I said to Catherine. Marsh is family, and so are you and David." His smile widened, and affection twinkled in his eyes. "More than that, I don't think Lily would ever forgive me if I let something happen to her David."

"He's attached to her too."

"It'll be good having more family close by. Relatively."

"We're looking forward to it." Levi's family was already large, but it never hurt to have more. Different support systems worked for different scenarios and different people. Levi had needed his parents and sisters and his cousin June after Kristin's death. David, it seemed, had needed a red-headed toddler and Marsh's moms, neither of which Levi could have predicted five weeks ago. "And looking forward to all this"—he gestured the direction of Helena's office—"being over."

"Helena's making her assessment. It will be over soon, one way or another."

A knock sounded at the door, and Levi twisted in his seat. Was it over already?

"Come in," Hawes called.

The door opened to one of the crew who'd arrived in San Diego with Helena three weeks ago, the person who'd had a rainbow mohawk at the time and had slipped Marsh the gate-number note. Today their hair was bright orange and their attire game-day ready—jeans, fleece, and orange and black Chucks. "You wanted to see me," they said.

"Jax," Hawes said. "Meet Levi Bishop, Marsh's husband. Levi, this is Jax."

"I'm sorry I didn't get to say hello at the airport," Jax said as they shook his hand. "And congrats. Marsh is awesome."

"Thanks, I think so too."

"Jax is one of Holt's hacker protégés," Hawes said as he moved to his desk chair, freeing up the other visitor one for Jax. "We've been going over what Marsh shared about Catherine's contacts, and we had some follow-up questions. The more variables we can control going into this exchange with Remy, the better."

"Let's do it." Levi didn't mind having the work to distract himself from whatever was going on two offices over. They'd been at it for over an hour when Helena poked her head into the office. "I'm going to show Catherine to the bunk. When are we leaving for the game?" she asked Jax.

"Cee and the kids will be here in thirty."

"That'll work. Gives me time to change. Got any idea when or where Remy will want to do this?"

"My guess on when, midday tomorrow," Jax said. "I've got one of her aliases on a flight out at four."

Helena glanced across the desk at her brother. "Where?"

"Given what Levi's told us about who she met with on her way to London, I'm going to guess the Hagan warehouse in South San Francisco."

"That tracks," Levi said. "Catherine said yesterday she'd have everything in place when Remy called."

Helena nodded. "Meaning money and transport."

"You should get some rest before then," Hawes said to Levi. "I'm guessing it's been a few days."

He started to count on his fingers and everyone laughed. "You got an extra bunk here?"

"How about an extra room at the house?" Helena said with that wink she was so fond of giving him.

"The house?"

The inviting warmth in Hawes's voice and eyes was the furthest thing Levi—hell, most anyone—would expect from the Prince of Killers. "You're family."

FOURTEEN

MARSH RARELY FLASHED his badge for personal reasons. He remembered as a kid his father flexing his standing as a professor to get what he wanted, usually lording it over this or that service person who he didn't think was moving fast enough. Or flexing his authority "as the breadwinner" over Camilla when he thought no one was listening. From what Marsh had overheard in Hanover, Jefferson had continued with his bad behavior, especially as his students had risen higher and carried his reputation higher with them.

Marsh refused to be like his father.

So he waited in line at airport ticketing like a good civilian, and once he got to the counter, he explained to the ticket agent he just needed the cheapest ticket that would get him back to the gates to pick up his son he hadn't seen in weeks and to please tell the gate agent he wouldn't be boarding so they didn't need to hold the plane for him or call his name God only knew how many times. She smiled, told him he was a good father, and thanked him for saving them the hassle. She also gave him a first-class upgrade so he could skip the ridiculously long security line full of summer tourists at San Diego's main airport, meaning he got to the gate Brax had texted him an hour early. He swept the area for any suspicious activity or packages, then stood by the plate glass windows and enjoyed the view. The only thing that marred the sunny San Diego morning was the bank of televisions reporting on a special announcement by California's own Representative Anthony scheduled for later that day. Speculation was rampant, most of it correct that he would be throwing his hat into the presidential primary ring. Some of the networks had gotten wind of Charles Sanders's remarks in Salzburg, but none of them, suspiciously, were reporting on the rest of that evening's excitement. Marsh smirked. News of the Sanders family drama and more would reach the masses soon enough.

The gate agent opened the jetway door to Marsh's right, and a few minutes later, one of the two private planes Marsh had become all too familiar with parked on the other side of the windows. It was barely another minute before Brax appeared at the door. Alone. Marsh tried not to let his smile fall, but judging by Brax's chuckle, he'd failed to hide his disappointment. "Not happy to see me, Major?" Brax said as they embraced.

"I'm always happy to see you. Just someone else I want to see more."

"He's here. I promise." Brax stepped back, his gaze roving the terminal. "Wanted to do a look around first."

"Got here an hour ago. Did a full sweep already."

"Good, maybe two sets of tired eyes are enough to make a pair of good ones."

Guilt spiked at the back-and-forth travel Marsh had put

his best friend through. "How much do I owe you and Mel in jet fuel?"

"Don't worry about it." Brax squeezed his shoulder, the corners of his mouth tipping up. "We'll collect when the time is right." He withdrew his phone and shot off a text. "They'll be out in a minute."

"Y'all staying?"

Brax shook his head. "Gotta get back. Holt will be running comms on the op, so I'm on Lily duty."

But if Holt and Lily weren't the other ones on the plane with David, then who were *they*? A guard may—

A familiar Texas drawl reached Marsh's ears. "So how far is the house from the water?"

"Close, I hope," another equally familiar voice said.

"Twenty minutes," David said. "Thirty in traffic," he told Marsh's moms who cleared the jetway behind him.

Marsh didn't have time to ask what was going on. David spied him and took off at a dead run. "Marsh!" He slammed into Marsh, who wrapped one arm around him and shot out the other to catch the cowboy hat that tipped off his head. David hugged him tight, and Marsh hugged him back tighter, dropping a kiss in his ginger mop of curls. His misty-eyed moms sighed. "Don't look at me like that," Marsh grumbled at them.

Camilla smiled, happiness beneath the teary sheen of her dark eyes. "The whole terminal is looking at you like that, mijo."

Irina looped an arm around her waist. "Good thing there's a ring on his finger."

David drew back enough to look up at him. "When is Dad getting here?"

"If all goes to plan, Wednesday." Maybe as early as

tomorrow, but Marsh was building in a cushion for Bureau admin. He didn't want to get David's hopes up. Better surprise than disappointment, especially with David's spirits so high, his smile as wide as Marsh had ever seen it.

He reclaimed his Stetson and flipped it back onto his head. "I want to show him my new hat."

Marsh eyed his mothers behind him. "Been spoiling him much?"

"Never," Camilla lied.

Everyone laughed, only reining it in when the gate agent who'd opened the jetway for Brax approached. "I'm sorry to interrupt, sir, but if you're going to keep your takeoff spot, we need to get you back on board."

"Thank you," Brax told her, then to Marsh and family, "That's my cue."

"You'll bring Lily to visit soon?" David asked. "I promised her ice cream from this amazing farmstand near Aunt Liz's place."

"Count on it." Brax hugged David goodbye, Marsh too, then kissed Camilla's and Irina's cheeks before he disappeared down the jetway, Irina humming appreciatively as he went.

Marsh rolled his eyes. "Stop it."

She shrugged, not the least bit ashamed. "I got spoiled with him around the ranch more."

Marsh made sure David had his bags, then grabbed the handles of his mothers' and started the group toward the exit. "Who's minding the ranch while you're gone?"

"Staff. Same as minded it when we visited you in Vienna."

"I think this is our first vacation since then," Camilla said.

"If their house is too far away from the water," Irina said, "we might have to think about that hotel room."

Camilla draped an arm over her shoulders and drew her into her side, voice low but still loud enough for them to hear. "We might think about it anyway."

David snorted and cut Marsh a side-eye. "I see where you get it from now."

Ignoring the two horny women, Marsh continued a step ahead with David. "You been practicing your chess between all the vet rounds?"

He nodded. "Brax showed me some moves too. I might be able to beat you now." He waggled his brows, and Marsh laughed out loud. David returned the smile, which grew wider as they stepped outside. He inhaled deep and turned his face up to the sun, gentler here than in Texas. "It's good to be home."

Marsh bumped his shoulder. "I couldn't agree more." Now he just needed to get Levi home with them too.

FIFTEEN

DAVID SAT OUTSIDE at the patio table, laptop open, earbuds in, gesturing animatedly to his father on-screen. From the kitchen, Marsh saw Levi's face, his smile stunning and bright, his gaze fixed lovingly on his son, only flitting away occasionally when Taco would cross into the frame behind David.

"This is the sweetest cat."

Marsh glanced over his shoulder and nearly dropped the knife he was using to slice and dice cucumbers. Camilla had entered the kitchen, Burrito in her arms, the tabby furball curled contentedly with its head tucked beneath his mother's chin. He set down the knife, wiped his hands, and snatched up his phone, snapping a picture.

"What was that for?" Camilla asked.

"No one would believe *that* cat allowed someone to hold her like *that* unless there's proof."

Camilla cooed at the usually grumpy beast. "It just takes the right someone, doesn't it, kitty?" She scratched behind the cat's ears, lulling her into purring slumber before

Camilla gently tucked her into the pile of blankets on the den couch. "Okay," she said, rejoining him in the kitchen. "What can I help with?"

"Peel and dice the avocados?"

"You got it." She washed her hands, grabbed a knife, and got to work across the island from Marsh.

"Irina okay?" Marsh asked. Camilla had come down alone, and he didn't hear Irina moving around upstairs.

"Yeah, just catching a nap. She and David have been running all over the county the past two weeks. As active as she is, she's a good bit older than his fourteen."

Marsh dumped the cucumbers into a colander, tossed them with salt, then placed the colander over a bowl to drain. "If this trip was too much—"

"This trip was the break we needed. Irina can't be on call from a thousand miles away." She snagged the cutting board and began dicing the peeled avocados. "And when you trusted David's safety to us, that didn't stop at the ranch gate."

His gaze skipped over her shoulder, checking on David outside, getting another shot of happiness seeing him healthy and whole, back at home. "Thank you for taking such good care of him."

"It was easy." She paused between avocados to gesture generally at their surroundings. "*This* is easy for you too, isn't it? You stepped over that threshold, and I don't think I've ever seen you so settled somewhere before. Not even at the ranch."

"I love Mi—"

"I know you do, mijo, and it will always be home, but this is your *home*."

Yes, that's how he'd come to think of it too. He'd been as

desperate to get back to it as David and Levi. But as eager as he'd been, Marsh had also been nervous, afraid the memory of how they'd left, of the near miss and frantic flight from danger, would overshadow the joy of returning, of the future he looked forward to here. But there'd been little time for nerves or fear last night as he and the team had secured the house. And no time for it today either, David's exuberance contagious and all-encompassing. He'd bustled in, dropped his bags, and launched right into giving Camilla and Irina a tour. So many of his highlights had included Marsh and so many of his references were prefaced with *our*. Marsh didn't think he meant only him and Levi. It all still seemed a little surreal, a miracle that the surly, reserved kid who had made it clear that first night that Marsh's presence was temporary had opened up to him over the board and now considered him a permanent fixture. Marsh had had to tread carefully. "It wasn't easy to start. I didn't want to step on the life Levi and David had here already, including the one they'd had with Kristin."

"But they made space for you."

"They did." Levi had offered him a home for a little while, then given him forever. He removed the colander from the bowl, dried the bowl out, then handed it to his mom to scrape the avocado into. "As for the house itself, the lingering sadness was unsettling at first, but there was so much love in these walls too. And when I stepped out onto that patio the first time…" He whistled, same as he had that night five weeks ago.

"Some view."

"Yeah." He squeezed a cut lemon over the avocado, added the cucumber, then tossed them with a spoon as his mind drifted back to that night. To Levi standing in the patio doorway, backlit by the setting sun, inviting him to see the view, inviting him into his and David's lives. Marsh had sensed he was in trouble already, but he'd known it for certain then.

"Aww," Camilla drawled as she rounded the island and hip-checked him out of the way of the fridge. "My love-struck baby boy. I knew it would happen one day."

She opened the fridge door just as David opened the patio one, laptop in hand, Taco at his heels. "Dad said he'll call you on your phone," he said to Marsh. "You're supposed to watch something together in five."

Marsh tapped his phone to check the time. How had it gotten to noon already? "I need to head up to the office."

Camilla set the pack of burgers on the counter. "We'll get working on these."

David groaned, still some of the surly teen left in him.

Which Camilla promptly batted down. "Wah-wah. Go start the grill."

"Was she always like this?" David asked him.

Marsh chuckled. "Pretty much." He was still laughing as he closed the office door and withdrew his phone, standing it next to his computer. He logged on and was just pulling up a live newsfeed when Levi's video call pinged. He answered it, and Levi's face filled the screen. There were bags under his blue eyes but not as bad as yesterday's, and his smile was as warm as Marsh had seen it since they'd left David in Texas. "Hey, you," Marsh greeted.

"Hey, yourself." He slumped onto what looked like the couch in Holt's attic lair at the Madigan mansion. The old Victorian had been home to three generations of Madigans. Helena and her family were now its primary residents, but the stately mansion remained the nonoffice hub of the

Madigan-Perri family and had room aplenty for guests. "How you doing?"

"Long night," Marsh replied, "but should be worth it here in a few." In addition to hours securing the house, there had also been hours of sorting and analyzing evidence from Greg and Amanda's crime scene. Most of it in real time as it had become available, all of it needed for the dominos that would soon start to fall. All their ducks had to be in a row. "How about you?"

Levi propped the phone on something and raked both hands through his hair. "A house full of assassins is not what I thought it would be like."

Marsh recalled the same feeling the first time he'd met the entire Madigan clan. He'd known Brax and Holt half his life, but it still hadn't prepared him. "It's like the family-friendliest place you can imagine, toys all over the place, and yet, there are elaborate comms systems and hidden weapons."

"Yes! Like this room." He waved a hand toward something off camera, the direction of Holt's wall of monitors. "And the food, ohmigod, the food."

"You sound like your son. Always the food."

Affection flooded his features once more. "He sounded so good, Marsh. Happy to be home but that it was a good hideout masquerading as a vacation."

"And he brought Texas home with him."

"He told me. San Francisco might be there too, based on Lily's to-do-with-David list. She spent all of dinner going through it with me."

"Your son is being corrupted."

"Pretty sure you're right, and I'm good with that. I'm just—" His voice cracked, and he glanced away, swallowing hard. When that didn't work to gather his composure, he tipped down his face and laced his hands behind his neck.

Marsh would have given anything to reach through the screen and wrap him in a hug. "Baby."

He lifted his chin, and the corners of his eyes were wet. "I'm just so glad he's happy again. And so fucking relieved. I was worried I'd lost him." He dropped his hands, straightened, and physically gave himself a shake. "Thank you for making us both happy."

Scratch that. Marsh wanted to reach through the screen and kiss him. "Me? I'm the one who was just downstairs telling my mom how happy I am that you two made space for me in your lives and your home."

"*Our* home, and I am so ready to be back there with you."

"Any idea when the op will go down?"

"Soon," Levi said. "Remy is on a flight out at four, so between now and then."

"Maybe she's waiting on this," Marsh said as Stewart Anthony appeared on the steps of his DC townhouse. His press secretary approached the podium first, laid down the ground rules, then turned the mic over to the congressman.

Levi shifted on the couch toward the wall of monitors and turned up the volume. "Here we go."

Anthony said all the right, awful words to energize and excite his supporters about the exploratory committee he was forming to assess a possible run for president.

"*Possible* my ass," Marsh mumbled. Charles hadn't said anything Friday night in Salzburg that had sounded remotely like *exploratory* or *possible*.

"Firm announcements are usually held until after the midterms," Levi said. "So formalities and all that."

The assembled press weren't buying it any more than Marsh or Levi. They skipped right over the exploratory bit and started asking when an official announcement would be made, who Anthony was considering as a running mate, and what the pillars of his platform would be.

"Fear and greed about cover it," Levi said.

"Don't forget war," Marsh added, recalling his interview with Stefan Sanders. "Whatever country he can pick a fight with fastest."

But someone else was there today to pick a fight with Anthony. "Excuse me, Representative Anthony." The crowd parted to reveal Charlie's boss, SAC Sutton Conder. He cut quite the camera-ready figure, his fit frame in a tailored gray suit that matched his dusting of early-forties gray hair.

"Sutton's doing this himself?" Levi gasped. "I thought we were leaking info to the press."

"As much as Anthony has a hard-on for the presidency, Sutton has a hard-on for taking him down." The SAC of the Criminal Investigative Division's organized crime unit was a notorious stickler for the rules—Sean had not been a fan of his when he'd been an agent—but Sutton had been an excellent boss, according to Charlie, and when it came to Anthony, he seemed willing to break all the rules.

"There's backstory there," Levi said. "Gotta be."

Judging by the way Anthony blanched, Levi probably wasn't wrong. "What are you—" Anthony started, only to be cut off by Sutton who cut right to the chase.

"Would you care to comment on the deaths of your associates, Greg Hudson and his daughter Amanda Hudson? They worked at the Sixth Avenue Shelter in San Diego. Your pet funding project. Greg was the assistant director and Amanda the programs coordinator."

Anthony contorted his features into confusion and surprise with just the right amount of practiced grief. "Greg and Amanda are dead? This is the first I'm hearing this terrible news." If anyone bothered to look at his hands clutching the podium, they'd notice his knuckles were white. "I'll—"

Sutton interrupted him again. "They were murdered, execution style."

Pandemonium erupted. Members of the press shouted at Anthony for answers and at Sutton for an ID. Anthony shouted at security to get Sutton out of there. The poor press secretary shouted at everyone to stop shouting.

Marsh's phone rang with another call, Charlie's name on-screen. He turned down the TV and turned his attention back to Levi. "That's Charlie."

"I'm guessing your afternoon is about to get a lot more interesting."

"Probably not as interesting as yours. This is good for you too."

"Oh, I know." Levi's sly grin, the excitement in his blue eyes, was sexy as hell. "Catherine will be delighted, especially when she finds out we delivered this to her."

"Work it, baby." Marsh grinned. "Then get your ass home so you can sip tea while David and I play chess."

"It's a date."

SIXTEEN

JAX'S PREDICTION on the time had been correct. Levi had barely hung up with Marsh when Hawes appeared at the top of the stairs. "Catherine's meeting Remy at two. Hagan Transport in South San Francisco."

Hawes's prediction had been correct too. "Nice work," Levi said as he stood and tucked his phone away.

"Nope. All the credit goes to you, Marsh, and your team. You gave us the intel. We just triangulated it."

Ninety minutes later, Hawes pulled their SUV into the parking lot of the oddly deserted for a Monday transport warehouse. Levi reached for the passenger door handle, but Hawes halted him with a hand on his forearm. "Gear up first." He opened the middle console, then entered a code on the tiniest keypad Levi had ever seen—"Kid proof" Hawes explained—to access a second compartment underneath.

Levi's eyes widened at the variety of weapons and comm devices crammed into the small space, each of them neatly tucked in foam. "Someone was a Boy Scout."

retrieved a bottle of champagne and a stack of plastic flutes. She peeled off the foil and Levi held the glasses while she filled them up. Catherine took her first sip, then nearly spit it out when Aidan Talley strode through the front door with a cadre of agents behind him, all of them in FBI windbreakers.

"Agent Bishop," the Irishman said, hand extended. "Good to see you again."

Catherine's gaze snapped to him. "*Agent*? I thought—" Red slashed across her cheekbones. "You lied about the reinstatements."

"I did." Levi set his glass down. "SAC Talley is here to execute on the extradition order. We'll be adding a few more charges I suspect."

Catherine drained her glass, then tossed the cup aside. "Pretty fucking face, I should have never believed you." She cut a glare at the Madigans. "Dimitri Petrov never wanted to do business with me, did he?"

"Likely not," Hawes said.

On her heels, Catherine clutched for scapegoat straws. "I'll tell the whole world Remy Pak is a mole for the feds and that the Madigans cooperate with law enforcement too."

"You can," Helena said, "but everyone knows that about us already."

"As you yourself said," Hawes added, "my brother and I married LEOs." He jutted his chin at Levi. "And our family friends are too."

"As for Remy," Helena continued, "she's Dimitri's favorite. He probably knows she cooperates from time to time, but so long as it doesn't blow back on him, which it rarely does, he lets it go. She makes him more money than you ever could, so honestly, he's just as likely to kill you for spreading rumors that might get her killed."

Catherine paled, and Levi saw his opening, the one he'd been waiting for this entire time. The leverage he and Marsh had talked about last night. "Did you see Stewart's news conference, Catt?"

The nickname drew her gaze to him, shrewd and a little hurt. She shook her head.

"His announcement did not go as smoothly as planned. The spotlight is on him and not for the reason he wants. You have an opening, Catherine, to ruin both him and your uncle for good this time. And don't tell me you've given up your grudge because, after the past few days together, I know you well enough to know that would be a lie."

"Those other charges Agent Bishop mentioned…" Aidan said. "They're negotiable *if* you cooperate."

Her gaze never strayed from Levi's. "Why should I trust you after this bait and switch?"

"Because you were never mine and Marsh's target. Because you, like us, are pawns in Charles and Stewart's game. Aren't you tired of playing by their rules? Isn't it time you made them play by yours?"

SEVENTEEN

THE WAR ROOM Levi set up eighteen months ago for the human trafficking case that had started with a tip from his late wife had never been more crowded. Boxes were stacked in every corner, new ones marked evidence were lined up beneath the whiteboard, and file folders and supplies were strewn the length of the conference table. Laptops and devices were plugged into every outlet, and every seat except the one beside Marsh was taken. Marsh felt that open seat like a hole in his heart. None of them would be there if not for Levi's tireless efforts to bring the traffickers who'd stolen countless lives to justice. He'd put his own life and career on the line to do so.

Marsh spun the ring around his finger. Levi had put his heart on the line too. In all his years of service, Marsh could say with absolute certainty that he'd never known another person as brave as his husband. And with Levi's latest victory, it was left to Marsh, Julia, and the rest of the team to bring Levi and the case home.

On the same wavelength, Julia stood at the head of the

table, her dark eyes sweeping the length of it. She couldn't officially be named SAC until after the final phase of their plan, but inside these walls, she was at the helm. She'd spent most of yesterday and today conferencing with Cam and getting up to speed on what she'd missed at the office and on other matters. Those matters handled, she now turned her attention to this one. "All right, sitrep." Her gaze landed on Matt first. "Greg and Amanda. Where are we with local?"

"They're cooperating," he replied. "To them, the case looks like a no winner. Execution-style killings, zero evidence left at the crime scene, no direct surveillance."

"We haven't told them otherwise," Alyssa said. "They don't want a loser on their board."

"What's our jurisdictional hook?"

"The fake IDs and bitcoin laundering," Cam said. "We disclosed that much to local. All the more reason they don't want to touch this case with a ten-foot pole."

"Also the broader Eder and Orchard trafficking case," Marsh said. "We'd prefer not to disclose that part to local either, but we could if we need to make that pole twenty feet."

"Organized crime will also flex if we have to," Sutton said from across the table. The SAC's stunt at Anthony's presser that afternoon had caused a shitstorm as they'd intended. Before anyone could come down on them with disciplinary action, Sutton and Charlie had taken the Paxton jet from DC to San Francisco, where Charlie had joined Levi's team. Sutton had continued on to San Diego; safe haven with Julia, his former terrorist task force colleague. Being out of DC and out from under Justice's thumb bought Sutton and Charlie, and the broader team, a day or two max, so it was all hands on deck, at all hours, the clock well past nine now.

"How long will the juice last?" Julia asked.

"As long as you keep feeding me info to hit Anthony with," Sutton replied. "Because he will push back. I expect him to call for an oversight committee first thing tomorrow. His party doesn't control the House right now, so it'll mostly be for show, but it's still not the attention we want unless we have ammunition to fire back with."

Julia gestured to the rest of the team. "Give the man the goods."

Alyssa opened a folder in front of her. "Coroner confirmed time of death was between twelve and four Sunday morning." She pushed the coroner's report and autopsy photos forward. "Two gunshot wounds. No struggle."

Will pushed the crime scene report into the center of the table next. "Per CSU, the scene was clean. No prints, no hair, no tracks, no other trace evidence. It's clean."

"Professional," Matt concluded.

"Clean but for the actual bodies" Marsh said. "Because the professional hitman was interrupted." Everyone leaned forward in their seats. Marsh had the goods for them, armed with the information he and Farmer had gathered over the past few hours. "Once we had the coroner's estimation on time of death, we were able to narrow the surveillance window." He opened one of the folders nearest to him and Farmer and added two black-and-white photos to the center collection. "These surveillance stills are from a traffic cam two blocks from the scene." The photos were blurry, a back shot of a person in a hoodie getting into a nondescript SUV.

"Do we have a better picture?" Cam asked.

Marsh passed the baton to Farmer, who'd been the one to hack the money shot. "These"—he added two better resolved, full-color photos to the stack—"are from surveillance footage of the entry gate at the complex across from where the SUV was parked."

"Farmer parsed through dozens of wireless networks to ID the one controlling those cameras," Marsh said. "Anyone look familiar?"

Matt drew the pictures closer, his eyes narrowing briefly before the dark brows above them raced north. "Is that Blaine Anthony?" He lifted his gaze. "No fucking way."

"Yes fucking way." Marsh unveiled his last picture, a facial recognition match to Representative Anthony's son. "We think he was there to drop off the fake IDs Amanda ordered."

Farmer played out the rest of their theory. "Blaine then stumbled on the killer and hauled ass out of there."

Cam tapped the black-and-white photo. "Is that his car?"

"Not according to any registrations in his or his parents' names."

"He left going west," Marsh said. "We're pulling any and all accessible footage that direction. Hopefully we get a hit on the license plate or VIN."

"We get Blaine," Matt said, "maybe we get a description of the killer."

"That's the goal."

"Stay on it," Julia told them, then zeroed in on Marsh again. "Catherine status, go."

"Levi delivered." There hadn't been any doubt in

Marsh's mind that his husband would. He'd pulled off his part with flying colors. "Catherine is ours."

"Charlie is in San Francisco coordinating with Talley," Sutton said. "We'll have Catherine in San Diego by tomorrow morning. Anthony is scheduled to fly in midday and will hold meetings in the afternoon with his exploratory committee, lawyers, and bankers."

Cam's hissing cringe made the entire table laugh. "Bet he wishes he'd planned that for DC now."

"Yes and no," Matt replied. "Heard from the shelter director that Anthony already called about making an appearance. And I quote, 'to pay tribute to Greg and Amanda, the shelter's loyal servants.'" Matt's air quotes were equally hilarious. "The director refused the request."

"Doesn't mean Anthony won't still try," Will said. "He's gotta sell that he's innocent in all this."

"Charles is coming with him?" Alyssa asked.

Sutton nodded. "He's hosting a meet and greet for potential donors at a house Anthony rented in Rancho Santa Fe. He can't donate himself as a foreign national but he can rally his US contacts."

"We need an in," Julia said.

"I've got that," Marsh said, rubbing his hands together. He knew the queen of Rancho Santa Fe, and she'd be happy to have him on his arm for a night. "I'm sure Levi's aunt already has an invitation."

"Do her politics align?" Matt asked doubtfully.

"Not a chance in hell, but her wallet and address do."

"Good," Sutton said. "But you can't go." He landed another blow before Marsh could protest the first. "Neither can Levi. Not if we want to sell this."

"He's been selling it just fine," Marsh defended.

"Yes, but you've been back on the scene here. There's been enough FBI involvement in San Francisco for someone to assume they're involved there. The reinstatement cover could very well be burned. We can't depend on it any longer."

"So then how do you propose we sell this?" Julia said.

"The other folks involved in San Francisco." Sutton swung his gaze back to Marsh. "Your family. They have a way of getting folks out of custody. Catherine shows up on a Madigan arm, Charles will think she's made new allies. Should get her an audience with Charles. She can sell that it's a temporary reprieve."

Marsh couldn't argue Sutton's deduction as one, a fair assessment, and two, a viable alternative. "Once there, Catherine can pitch the Bratva deal to Charles."

"Do we think he'll bite?" Julia asked. "Levi teed us up. We have to close this."

Marsh couldn't agree more. He wouldn't let Levi's sacrifices go to waste. "Going on what Sutton said, if we arrest Catherine *after* she's told Charles about the Bratva deal, then Charles can swoop in, reestablish lines with the Bratva, and claim all the glory. It plays into the game he's playing with Anthony. It brings him one step closer to the outcome they want. He'll bite."

"And once he does?" Sutton prompted, the thinly veiled vengeance in his brown eyes unmistakable. He was as invested in this case as they were now.

"We use all this"—Marsh gestured at the table—"and Charles to capture the last piece left on the board. Anthony won't be a sitting congressman when this is over."

EIGHTEEN

BY TWO IN THE MORNING, Marsh threw in the towel. Too little sleep the however many nights before, plus settling the family back in at the house, plus settling himself back in at the office, plus another few hours reviewing surveillance footage once he'd returned home, and Marsh was done. He'd be no good to Levi or anyone in the morning without some real rest. He closed his laptop, tossed his glasses on top of it, and grabbed his phone off the charger. Standing, his bones and muscles protested, joints cracking all over. Then cracking some more when he jolted suddenly at the phone vibrating in his hand.

He glanced at the screen, and his pulse rocketed into his throat. The home security app reported motion at the curb. A half second later, a car door shut outside, muffled as if someone was trying to be quiet. Activity at this late hour was unusual for the neighborhood; this could not be good. Marsh tapped the banner notification to open the app, then set the phone on the nearby file cabinet so he could open the gun safe in the office closet.

The phone vibrated again. Fuck. Motion detected closer to the house. The new video loaded over the first one, and Marsh stopped midspin of the bolted safe door, not believing what his eyes were telling him. Connor, the Madigan guard who'd been assigned to Levi's family at Aunt Liz's and was now on the house, was halfway down the front walk, shaking hands with Levi. Marsh's pulse kicked up again, adrenaline of a different sort pumping through his veins.

He hustled out of the office, deactivated the house alarm, and barely caught himself from thundering down the stairs. He took them at a quieter pace, clearing the bottom step just as Levi opened the front door.

Questions fired inside Marsh's head. What was he doing there? Where was Catherine? What did this mean for the op? But as Levi dropped his bag and closed the door, as he turned and locked his tired eyes with Marsh's, none of Marsh's questions mattered anymore. All that mattered was Levi under the same roof as him. Under their roof. Home. And Marsh sure as fuck wasn't staying on his side of the room this time.

He closed the distance between them and claimed his husband's mouth. Despite the late hour and what had to be as little if not less sleep than Marsh, Levi caught right on, twining his arms around Marsh's neck and diving into the kiss with him. Marsh shuffled him back against the door and deepened the kiss, tongues tangling, bodies pressed together. As they reacquainted themselves with each other, as Levi plowed his fingers into Marsh's hair and Marsh swallowed his husband's whimpers, Marsh thought maybe this was his favorite kiss he and Levi had ever shared. Nothing hidden, souls and hearts bared, both of them on the same page, both of them relieved to be back together, exactly where they were meant to be.

"Welcome home," Marsh mumbled against Levi's lips.

Levi rested their foreheads together and sighed contentedly. "Fuck, you have no idea how good that sounds."

"Oh, but I do."

Levi gentled his fingers in Marsh's hair, carding them through it soothingly. "You sound good too."

"We keep talking and moaning and we'll wake the whole damn house up."

"Which is exactly what I was trying to avoid by sneaking in at this hour."

Marsh leaned back, unsurprised to find a smirk on Levi's face. "Bad Bishop."

He grinned, the dark circles under his eyes no match for the light in his eyes. "Let me peek in on David, then I want to spend the rest of the night with my husband before all hell breaks loose in the morning."

"Good to know I didn't lie to David. You actually are the smartest man I know."

Levi chuffed and playfully shoved his chest, creating enough room to slip out from between him and the door. Marsh stifled the laugh that wanted to bubble free, and while Levi tiptoed down the hall toward David's domain, Marsh leaned his head outside to thank Connor before closing the door and locking everything back up. He grabbed Levi's bag, checked that Taco and Burrito were still snoozing in the den, then headed upstairs. He swung by the office to finish locking things up there, then crossed the catwalk to the master. He was in the bathroom, splashing water on his face to wake himself the rest of the way up when he heard the bedroom door shut. He straightened, dried his face with a hand towel, and could hardly believe his eyes still when Levi appeared in the mirror behind him. Could hardly contain his heart from beating out of his chest when his husband's arms wrapped around him from behind.

"I know it wasn't that long apart," Levi mumbled between his shoulder blades. "But it felt like too long."

"We're newlyweds." Marsh tossed the towel on the vanity and laid his hands over Levi's, their rings softly clanking. "We're not supposed to be apart."

"You're pretty smart too."

He chuckled and leaned into the warm body behind his, enjoying the quiet moment, matching his breaths to Levi's, then after a minute, noticing them getting longer.

He drummed his fingers over the back of Levi's hands. "How do you want to play this? You must be beat."

Levi snuggled closer. "But you just said we're newly-weds." He snuck a hand out from under Marsh's and aimed it lower, coming to rest over Marsh's bulge.

Levi stroked his cock through the thin material of his athletic shorts, and fuck, that felt good, but did tired or horny win? "If you need to sleep…"

"After sex," Levi said, answering Marsh's question.

"Not gonna argue."

"I can feel that." Levi stroked him once more, then unfortunately—or thankfully—let up on the torture. He brought his hands higher, splaying them over Marsh's chest and holding him snug while directing him toward the bedroom. His hands didn't stay put for long, though, stripping Marsh as they walked. Pushing his T-shirt up and off and dappling kisses across Marsh's bare back and shoulders. Shoving his shorts and boxers down, hands cupping his ass cheeks as they reached the side of the bed. Skating his fingers over Marsh's hips and diving into the vee of his pelvis.

Marsh hung his head back on a curse that turned to a moan when Levi licked into the crook of his neck and raked his nails down Marsh's chest. Marsh shivered. The soft and rough handling and the fact Levi was still fully dressed behind him was driving Marsh wild. And bringing his cock to full attention. "You're wearing too many clothes."

Levi nipped his earlobe. "So turn around and sit on the bed while I strip." He gave him another playful push, and Marsh managed to spin just before he crashed onto the bed.

And what a view he had in front of him. His husband, at home again, in their bedroom, stress drained from his limbs, eyes bright with lust and love. Levi kicked his shoes off into the corner, bent to remove his socks, and threw those into the corner too. Straightening, he undid his belt and fly, lowered his jeans and boxers, and stepped out of them. Then, two hands over his head, he pulled his shirt up and off, doing that sexy thing where all his muscles bunched and flexed in all the right places. It wasn't a show per se, but it was the very thing Marsh needed. A cherished glimpse into their future. Countless nights ahead to casually undress in front of each other, to share each other's space, to just hold each other and breathe.

He reached out, snagged Levi's hand, and drew him forward. Levi didn't resist. He climbed onto the bed and straddled Marsh's lap. Marsh lifted a hand and brushed his hair off his forehead. "What do you need tonight?"

"To be with you." A coyote howled outside, drawing Levi's gaze over his shoulder toward the open window. "Should we close the curtains?"

Marsh shifted his hand, thumb tracing one of Levi's moonlight-kissed cheekbones. "You know I love you like this, all wolfed out." He tipped his own head the direction of the window. "I want to take you there."

"The canyon?" Levi asked with a smirk.

Marsh gave his ass a pat for the sass. "In front of the window."

"Now?"

He shook his head. As tempting as that sounded, tonight wasn't the time for that fantasy. "When we both have the energy to stand for more than ten minutes and when there's no one else in this house so I can make you scream."

Goose bumps prickled Levi's skin all the way down to the curve of his ass. "How would you do that?"

"I'd tell you to spread your arms and legs." He hitched Levi more firmly onto his lap, spreading his knees and thighs farther apart and bringing their stiff pricks into contact. "I'd tell you to press your palms to the glass that had been warmed by the sun all day." He hauled Levi even closer, their erections pressed snug together. "Your cock too." He rocked his hips, and Levi rocked back, the friction divine. "You'd be shoved up against that warm glass while I tongue fucked your hole."

"Marsh, fuck." He shifted so he could rest his forehead on Marsh's shoulder, and with the narrow space created between them, reached a hand down and grasped their cocks together in his fist.

"There's my smart husb—"

Levi swiped a thumb over his head, stealing Marsh's words and collecting the moisture there. Spreading it and his own precome over them. "Keep going. Tongue fucking."

"Right." He held Levi close, braced with one hand on his back while Marsh brought the other to his mouth. He sucked two fingers, a bit of a show for Levi, who groaned and stroked them faster. Faster still when Marsh brought his wet fingers to the cleft of Levi's ass. "How long could you last, Levi?" He slid his fingers lower, circling his rim. "How long could you hold all that come in while I speared your hole with my tongue?" He pressed the tip of a finger inside. "Or would you rather have my cock?"

Levi keened and rocked harder, riding Marsh's hand as his own continued stroking them together.

"I'd still be dressed," Marsh said. "Standing behind you with just my cock out. You'd be naked, all this pale skin glowing in the moonlight, your eyes all wolfy."

"Marsh."

"What would I feel like against you?" Marsh roughly palmed his ass cheek. "The denim against your thighs…"

"Rough."

Marsh tilted slightly back, bringing more of their bodies into contact. "My shirt against your skin."

"Soft." Levi bent an arm over his shoulder and splayed his hand over Marsh's delts. "Hot from your skin underneath."

"My cock."

Levi groaned in his ear, breath so hot Marsh nearly combusted. "Hard."

"Slick."

"Messy."

"That's right, baby." Marsh curled a hand over Levi's around their cocks. Jerking them off together. "We'd make a mess. Me ramming my cock inside you. You smearing the window."

"Together."

"You and me, Levi." He kissed a path along his cheekbone. "Just the moon and the coyotes."

Levi stiffened, on the verge of orgasm. "And anyone across the canyon with a telescope."

Marsh was right there too, his balls drawing up. "Do you know what they'd see, Levi?"

"Everything," Levi groaned as he jerked in Marsh's arms, his come covering their fists.

"Yeah, baby." Marsh stroked them twice more, his grip come-slick and warm. Perfect. "Everything I promised to give you."

Levi's "Yes" against his lips ended Marsh's wait, pushing him over the edge. He exploded in his husband's arms, right where he wanted to be. At home.

NINETEEN

"WHY DO I SMELL PEPPERMINT?" David trudged through the open dog gate in his SDSU sweats, the hoodie opening cinched tight around his face, his freckled skin and ginger brows clashing wildly with the school's scarlet and black. Eyes closed, nose scrunched, runaway curls sneaking out from under the hood, he was the much-missed picture of grumpy morning teen.

Biting back a laugh, Levi glanced at Marsh to make sure he had his phone ready. He nodded, and Levi, standing beside the island, answered David's question. "Because I refuse to drink Marsh's bean water."

David's eyes popped open, comically wide for how tightly shut they'd been a second ago. "Dad?"

The picture snap sounded. "Got it," Marsh said.

David scrubbed his hands over his face, dislodging the hood from his head. "Am I dreaming?"

"Nope," Camilla said from where she stood in front of the oven, engaged in a standoff with Taco over who would lay claim to the goodness inside. "That's really him."

David didn't hesitate, zipping across the room and into Levi's open arms. Levi hugged his kid, no better feeling in the world. David was safe, Marsh was safe, he was safe. His whole world was back together under one roof, breakfast as usual. "When did you get here?" David asked.

"Oh dark thirty."

"You snuck in is what you did," Irina said from her spot at the breakfast table. Maybe not exactly usual.

Marsh moved around her, gathering plates and silverware. "What of it?"

David drew the rest of the way back. "Marsh said you wouldn't be back until tomorrow."

"We thought later today was a possibility." Marsh placed the stack of tableware on the end of the bar closest to the patio door. "But we didn't want to get your hopes up in case it slipped to tomorrow."

Marsh stepped closer, and Levi snaked an arm around his waist. He snuggled into Marsh's side and kissed the hinge of his scruffy jaw. "I surprised him too."

"Gross, no." David covered his face again. "I don't wanna know."

Chuckling, Levi lightly grasped one of his son's wrists and drew it down. David opened one eye, peeking for safety, and judging the coast clear, lowered his other hand and opened that eye too. "Go set the table outside," Levi told him. "Your other grandparents will be here shortly. And take Taco with you so Camilla can actually get into the oven."

David spun the direction of the oven, nose finally getting the better of him. "Is there breakfast casserole in there?"

Levi used the wrist still in his to redirect him. "You. Taco. Outside. Go."

He sighed dramatically. "It's like you don't even want to see me."

"Nothing could be further from the truth." He drew David close and dropped a kiss on his head. "I've been down here an hour waiting to hug you. Two weeks if we're counting."

"I know." He leaned into Levi, another brief hug, before rotating toward the end of the bar with the dishes. "I'm just giving you shit."

"Language," Levi and Marsh corrected together. They were summarily ignored; that much was usual.

Once he was outside, Irina stood and refilled her and Levi's mugs of tea from the French press. "Is you being home early a good or bad sign?"

"Good. We had some breaks go our way."

"Because you are damn good at your job." Marsh squeezed his shoulders and kissed his temple, then circled behind the island to retrieve a bowl of fruit salad from the fridge.

"What do you need us to do today?" Camilla asked as she removed the breakfast casserole from the oven and placed it on a trivet beside the fruit salad on the island.

"Continue distracting him," Levi said with a head tilt David's direction. "And my parents. They know I'm an agent, and Dad was career military, but I think they're still rattled from our mad dash out of here." During each check-in call Levi had had with them, there'd been a wobble of worry in his mom's too many words and concern in his dad's too few words, even for the quiet man he was.

"I have a list of things I want to see in town," Irina said before a smirk turned up one corner of her mouth. "Starting with Coronado."

"Top of my list too," Camilla said. "Our boy had to go and join the army." She hip-checked Marsh out of the way of the serving spoon drawer. "Couldn't do the nice thing for his mothers and join the navy."

"Hey!" Marsh pointed a spoon at Irina. "The army got you Brax."

Levi laughed, their humorous back-and-forth something he would never tire of. Would amuse the heck out of his parents too. "Mom and Dad were born and raised in San Diego. If it's on your list, they'll make it happen." Right on time, the doorbell rang. "That'll be the military-prompt San Diegan's now." He headed toward the door, momentarily waylaid by Marsh, who stole a kiss. The bell had just rung again when Levi opened the door to his parents. "Hey, Mom and Dad."

Margaret didn't say anything, just threw herself into his arms and hugged him tight. He returned the embrace, reminded again how lucky he was to be home and have such loving, understanding parents. He patted his mom's back. "Thank you for rolling with things the past few weeks. I know it wasn't easy."

Beside them, his dad clasped his shoulder. "You've rolled with things your whole life, son. It was our turn."

His mom leaned back and wiped her eyes. "Everything's good now?" Then swept her thumbs under his eyes. When the bags there didn't magically disappear, a divot formed between her brows. "You look like you haven't slept."

"I've still got some catching up to do."

"And I'll make sure he does." Marsh joined them in the great room and hugged Margaret while Levi gave his dad a hug too.

"But are things good?" she asked Marsh too. "Truly?"

"Getting there on the work front." He hugged Tom next, then drew Levi to his side again, an arm over his shoulders while Levi looped one around his waist. "But here," Marsh said, "we're good and happy to be home."

Levi's mom smiled, relief audible in her sigh and visible in her frame that released its worried tension. And then her nose twitched, so much like David's that Levi laughed out loud. She swatted him for it. "What is that smell? It's absolutely divine."

"My mom's breakfast casserole." Marsh untangled himself from Levi's hold, only to slip an arm through the crook of Margaret's elbow and aim her toward the kitchen. "Come on, let me introduce you."

Levi trailed behind at a slower pace with his father. "You mind playing tour guide today?"

Tom shook his head. "Not at all. You know I love showing folks around town. Will Connor be with us?" Levi nodded. His family had become familiar with the Madigan guard during the hide-in at Liz's mansion, which was good. They knew and trusted him. But his presence still spun a thread of doubt his dad couldn't shake. "Are things really getting there?"

"We've made headway," Levi told him. "We'll know a lot more after tonight."

"You need David to stay with us?"

It wasn't a bad idea, depending on how the op went.

"Thank you. We should be back home tonight, but we'll keep you posted." There was raucous laughter from the kitchen just as they neared the gate. "Fair warning, David comes with two more grandmas now."

Tom snickered. "I kept your mother from murdering her sister for two weeks. I think I can handle it."

TWENTY

MARSH HAD BEEN RIGHT. Aunt Liz was the queen of Rancho Santa Fe, and she knew everything there was to know about Representative Anthony's donor event. The food and drinks on the menu, the guests and local celebrities invited, and most importantly, the floor plan of the house where the event was being held less than a mile away. Marsh glanced at the time on his computer screen. In less than an hour too.

"Okay, let's go through it one more time," Levi said from the head of Liz's monster dining table. She'd also graciously let them use her home as a staging area for tonight's operation.

"Sutton and Charlie will coordinate central from here," Marsh said. "Matt and Cam will be a block away with a field team in case reinforcements are needed. Levi, Farmer, Julia, and I will be listening in from a mock catering van outside the target location. Hawes"—Marsh nodded to the eldest Madigan across the table—"netted an invite to the event and will escort Catherine." Hawes tapped the Pride pin on his suit jacket lapel and the tiny bug inside transmitted video and audio to Marsh's laptop. "Reading loud and clear."

"How are you selling this?" Sutton asked Hawes. "If Levi's aunt's politics didn't align, yours certainly don't. Your family publicly funds LGBTQ teen shelters and causes."

Hawes counted off on his fingers. "We're also small business owners, high net-worth, and politically active on veterans' affairs, which we already know Anthony intends to make a platform issue." He wriggled a fourth finger, his pinky. "Opposition research, if the congressman really wants to push me."

Marsh didn't think anyone in their right mind would push Hawes Madigan, and if someone was too oblivious to pick up on the assassins don't-push-me signals, then there was no help for them. "Right," Levi said, reaching the same conclusion. "Carry on, Marsh."

"Hawes will make an excuse to speak to Anthony so Catherine can speak to Charles alone. Catherine will tell Charles she's reopened channels with the Bratva and that she took receipt of a shipment of weapons the Hagans are transporting. The Bratva expect to receive the shipment on this end Thursday so they can deliver it to the cartel in exchange for women and drugs, which the Bratva will split with EC."

"How was she paid?" Charlie asked from her seat beside Sutton.

"NFTs," Farmer replied. "She can show her uncle the accounts and activity. I set all that up with Frederick. Looks like laundering business as usual, just a different currency so to speak."

TWENTY-ONE

"SHE'S GOOD," Marsh said from beside Levi in the surveillance van. They were watching and listening through Hawes's Pride pin and Catherine's hair clip as they worked the crowd at the donor event. The duo easily slipped in and out of conversations, smoothly engaging with Anthony's potential donors, all while making steady progress to where Anthony and Charles were holding court near the center of the room.

"She was like this all the way across Europe," Levi said. "She didn't climb the corporate ladder on crimes and nepotism alone. Hawes is good too." Tonight's Mr. Madigan was not the icy assassin Levi had seen interact with Remy and Catherine nor the reserved strategist from their preop meetings. Tonight, he was warm and inviting, closer to the man who'd called Levi family and opened the family home to him.

"His grandparents were major players in San Francisco, legit and otherwise," Marsh said. "Hawes watched and learned and was ready to take over both aspects of the business. He plays better with others than Helena, who plays better with knives, and Holt would rather play with his computers, so…" He gestured at the screen where a smiling Hawes was shaking hands with an older gentleman.

Levi chuckled. "Makes sense when you put it that way." They continued to watch Hawes and Catherine close in on their targets. Charles spied his niece first, the moment obvious. He and Anthony were speaking to a couple about water shortages in drought-prone areas, Charles's accented voice distinctive, when he stopped midsentence, startled silent.

Anthony noticed the abrupt halt and begged the potential donors' forgiveness. "Charles, what—" His gaze tracked the direction of Charles's, his words likewise dying when the crowd parted for Catherine and Hawes to approach.

"Showtime," Marsh murmured.

Hawes hung back and let Catherine lead. Her bearing, her smile, the warmth she so expertly faked was chilling. She leaned forward and kissed her uncle's cheeks. "Uncle Charles, it's so good to see you."

Anthony recovered faster, his game face in peak performance mode tonight. "Catt, what a lovely surprise." He returned the cheek kiss she offered, and while close, whispered in her ear, "And since everyone was searched at the door, I know we're safe tonight." He leaned back and smiled the smile of a politician out for every vote. "I'm sorry we didn't get to spend more time together last week."

Catherine, to her credit, didn't miss a beat. "I'm sorry too. We're all so busy. Any time with family is a gift. This opportunity presented itself, and I couldn't say no to seeing you both again."

Charles finally found his words. "Catherine, I thought you were—"

"In San Francisco." Hawes stepped to her side, hand extended to Charles first. "Hawes Madigan." Then to Anthony. "Catherine and I had mutual interest in being here tonight, so I made it happen."

Charles remained circumspect, clearly knowing something of the Madigans. Anthony too, though his approach was more direct. "I must say, Mr. Madigan, when I saw your name on the guest list, I was surprised. Even more surprised to learn Catherine was your plus one." His gaze flickered to the Pride pin, and thinly veiled contempt flared in his eyes. A straight person probably wouldn't recognize it; a queer person would. Levi did, so did Marsh judging by the tension that visibly rippled through him, settling in his too-tight shoulders. Levi laid a hand on his thigh while on-screen, Anthony continued to needle Hawes. "Where's your husband?"

"At the Giants game with his niece and nephew," Hawes answered, perfectly pleasant. How he kept the coolness out of his voice, Levi would never know.

"What sort of mutual interests brought you here?" Charles asked, maneuvering more carefully around this newest piece on the board.

"Representative Anthony made veterans' affairs a centerpiece of his last campaign," Hawes explained. "Our family has a vested interest, especially as it concerns PTSD and mental health."

Contempt fled Anthony's eyes, dollar signs flashing there instead. Fucking asshole. "Our veterans face so many challenges after discharge, reentering the workforce at the top of that list."

Marsh cursed. "Always the almighty dollar. When I got out, I just wanted to sleep through the night."

Dual *Amen*s echoed behind them, Julia and Farmer, the other two vets in the van sharing Marsh's sentiment.

"Stewart," Catherine said. "Do you mind if I have a word in private with my uncle?" She played the role of doting niece to perfection. Could Anthony really say no in a crowd full of people without raising suspicions? Charles seemed to recognize the same, saving Anthony the trouble with a nod.

"Mr. Madigan." Anthony gestured toward the nearest bar. "Let's grab a drink and chat further."

The crowd swallowed them up, and moments later, the right side of Marsh's laptop screen went fuzzy. "We lost Madigan," Sutton radioed from command. "Audio and video were cut."

"Stay on Catherine," Marsh said. "Hawes can take care of himself." He closed the right half of the split screen so Catherine's feed was the only one visible.

Levi spun half-around in his chair. "See if you can restore Hawes's feed," he said to Farmer.

The cyber agent nodded, and Levi rotated back in time to see Charles and Catherine in what looked like a parlor room. "What happened to your pet FBI agent?" Charles snapped.

The view from Catherine's hair pin tilted up, indicating her face had too, Charles looming over her. But Catherine held her ground. "I decided Hawes was a better bet."

"Better bet for what?" His voice dripped with judgment, only the lowest grades for his traitorous niece.

"For connecting me to the Bratva. The Madigans are tight with Remy Pak."

way into the room and lowered himself into the chair beside Marsh. "Thank you all for helping to make this happen."

"The case is officially yours again," Julia said, then jutted her chin at the donuts. "You also get first dibs."

"For the record," Cam said, "I didn't agree to that part."

Matt swatted his friend and former partner. "Of course you didn't. You always gotta get the first Dunkin'."

"What part of Boston"—Cam gestured at himself—"did you not understand?"

Levi laughed the rest of the lump in his throat away. "All right, someone pass me a blueberry glazed and let's play this next part out."

Boxes were opened, donuts descended upon, and once everyone was settled with their fried dough of choice, Charlie kicked them off. "Catherine is in custody."

"Quietly, as we agreed," Sutton added. "She made her one phone call—to Charles."

"He in turn reached out to the Hagans," Marsh reported. "Then to an attorney for Catherine."

"He was smart enough not to ask for my sister," Hawes said as he tore his strawberry-frosted donut into bite-sized pieces. Levi bit back a smile, remembering the same reflex action from when David was a toddler, even if it was food for himself.

"Remy still on track for arrival?" Marsh asked.

"She's flying down from Seattle tonight." He munched on a bite. "Will be at the Hagan facility in Poway tomorrow after hours. Victoria and Avery have been following the shipment. They'll front as Remy's crew, then deliver the weapons into your custody."

Levi set his remaining half donut aside and confessed

the truth he—none of them—could escape, especially after Catherine's pitch to Charles last night. "It seems too easy."

Relief crested like a wave around the table and crashed beside him, Marsh letting out a giant exhale. "Thank fuck someone else said it."

Julia chuckled. "Which is why we have to be prepared for it to go sideways. Likely scenarios?"

"Charles is a no show," Will said. "He either changes his mind or directs the Hagan transport elsewhere."

"We'll know on the latter," Hawes said. "And if he bails on the Bratva, he's a fool."

"And if he tries to flee," Sutton said, "he's on the TSA watch list."

"We also left eyes on Anthony's rental," Farmer said, "where Charles is also staying. We'll know if he detours."

Julia nodded, seemingly satisfied with the guardrails for the scenarios suggested. "Next."

"Remy brings in someone else *she* trusts to actually take the weapons," Cam threw out.

Alyssa swerved a slightly different direction. "Or Charles brings in someone to rip them off."

All were scenarios Levi and Marsh had considered last night when reviewing area maps. "We've got several nearby retail lots we can stage in." Pushing to his feet, he nodded to Marsh who displayed the maps they'd worked up on the conference room screens. "Once the weapons are confirmed on-site, we'll set up roadblocks here, here, and here." He pointed to choke points on Community, Stowe, and the Scripps Poway Parkway.

Alyssa stood and approached the other side of the screen, tapping the SPP roadblock. "If they get past this one and onto the 15, it's a straight shot to the 805 and the border."

"We'll alert border patrol as well," Sutton said.

"Any others?" Julia said.

Levi stepped away from the screen and leaned against the back of his chair. "Catherine engineers the rip-off."

Marsh rotated his direction. "The wildcard."

He nodded. "It's a more likely scenario than Charles or Remy, and she told us as much last night. I don't think she was lying about the *we can't let the feds take this* part. Take her at face value on that. The lie in what she told Charles was the *we*. She won't let anyone win but her."

"We'll lob a call into Wagner, Ross, and Binny," Marsh said. "Have them go back through her Salzburg to London contacts. See if there's movement anywhere."

"There will be." Levi glanced again at the screen. "Containment plan still applies." Then grimaced. "With Catherine, though, the need to keep things discreet does not."

"Downer," Marsh grumbled.

"We gotta be prepared," Julia said. "Including worst-case scenarios."

Marsh leaned back in his chair, the springs squeaking. "Hey, can't be as bad as watching a building come down on our friends, right?"

"Or," Cam said as he reached for the leftover Boston Kreme donut, "having the man you love kidnapped right out from under your nose with only donuts left behind."

Hawes rubbed a hand over his chest. "Or having to shoot the man you love and push him into the Bay."

"Sorry, y'all," Charlie said with a raised hand. "I got this one. Serial killer who thinks I'm Lady Macbeth and tries to murder me in front of my sister on the bridge where our mother died."

"Oof," Farmer said, "I think we have a winner."

"Or," Sutton spoke quietly, eyes on no one, as he threaded a finger under his shirt collar and withdrew a thin silver chain, idly weaving it through his fingers, "letting the man you love go to jail for a crime he didn't commit so you can keep your shiny brass badge."

The table was quiet almost long enough to be awkward, but their Boston visitor saved them, reaching forward to shove the Dunkin' box Sutton's direction. "You win the last donut prize."

Even Sutton chuckled at that, as did the rest of the table, the tension dissipating.

"You see what you did, Agent Bishop?" Julia said. "Bringing all this bad luck up in here."

He glanced to his left, to the handsome cowboy who met his eyes. Bad luck, maybe, but with a heaping side of love and hope. And friends aplenty, where just weeks ago, even in his own office and around his own family, loneliness dominated. "Worth it."

TWENTY-THREE

"SO, Levi, what's after this case for you?" Cam took another swig from his bottle of Imperial Stout, casual like, not like he'd just plucked from Marsh's head the question that had been swirling at the back of it all day, ever since Levi had strode back into the Bureau war room. Once he'd gotten over his initial surprise, he'd settled right back in like he belonged there.

Julia balled up a napkin and threw it at the San Francisco ASAC. "Stop trying to steal my best agent."

"Hey!" Marsh protested in time with Matt's, "What about the rest of us?"

Levi just laughed and sipped his IPA. He was snuggled against Marsh's side, the two of them tucked into the corner of one of the outside lounge areas at Pacific Heights Brewing.

"Marsh will back my play, won't you?" Cam cajoled. "Your best friend lives in San Francisco. Wouldn't you love to be in the same city as him?"

"He does, and I would, but even so, you want us to give

up this perfectly gorgeous July weather"—he gestured vaguely with his own bottle at their surroundings, a very pleasant seventy-something degrees at nine o'clock at night —"for cold summer fog?" Marsh shook his head. "Nope, not even for Brax."

Cam pretended to sulk until Matt knocked him sideways with his shoulder, their laughter contagious. Their chuckling server dropped off a second round of appetizers, and it was only after they demolished most of the food that Sutton picked up the thread again. Not surprising as he was frequently on the Bureau's hiring team, his assessment of folks rarely wrong. See Charlie, who made an excellent agent. "But seriously, Levi, where do you see your career with the Bureau going?"

Levi's body against Marsh's remained relaxed, a good sign. A month ago, he would have tensed, worried about his job and keeping a roof over his and David's heads. Marsh would be forever grateful he'd had the opportunity to take that stress off Levi's shoulders. "I need to be home with my son more," Levi said. "It was a rough two years after his mom died. He's doing better now, but I don't want him to backslide while we're not watching."

Hearing Levi say *we* when discussing their future, parenting David together, would never get old. Marsh was happily rolling around in those feels when Julia knocked him—and Levi—for another loop. "I need an ASAC," she said.

"I wouldn't make a good ASAC," Levi replied. Marsh opened his mouth to object, but Levi was already offering up another option. "Matt would make a better political player. He's better at hiding the ball when he needs to."

"Sorry, bro," Matt said as he finished the last bite of dirty fries. "I put in a transfer request to LA last week."

"Like that!" Levi said, though he didn't seem half as surprised as Marsh, who gasped a "What?"

"I've got family there," Matt explained. "This case has made me realize I should spend more time with them." His last words were barely audible over the fighter jet that thundered overhead. "And those fucking things are driving me fucking nuts. It's nine at night for fuck's sake."

Levi snickered. "I'll miss you, but I knew that day at Celome that you probably weren't going to make it here. You're not the first friend those planes have chased off."

Marsh didn't miss how Levi snuggled closer. He tipped his head to whisper in his husband's ear. "You don't have to worry about me and the planes."

The first jet's wingman zoomed overhead, distracting everyone else while Levi gazed at him with that soft unguarded smile that made Marsh's heart race. "Knew that too that first night you stayed at our place. You just fit here." He clasped Marsh's free hand and threaded their fingers together. "And with us."

While they'd been making heart eyes at each other, their colleagues had apparently been plotting the hard sell. "You'd make a great ASAC, Levi," Sutton said. "You've got the tactical mind for it, and you can make trafficking even more of a focal point for the office, which organized crimes will not complain about."

"Everyone in the office looks up to you," Matt said.

Followed by Cam's, "They couldn't stop asking about you until you were back."

Julia swooped in for the close. "And it's a desk job."

"You haven't been at your desk much lately," Levi countered.

"My fault," Marsh admitted. "But before this case she was. Mostly."

"I'm not saying to ignore the private sector," Julia said. "Feel it out, but just know the Bureau, our office, and I would hate to lose you."

Levi quietly sipped his beer, considering, while Sutton shifted his attention to Marsh. "What about you?"

Marsh suspected Sutton cared less about him than Levi as a long-term Bureau asset, but he was smart enough to rope Marsh into helping sell Levi on the ASAC position. Marsh didn't object to the idea or to being used in this case. He couldn't imagine a place where he'd be happier, at home with Levi and David and in the office with Levi, Julia, and colleagues he respected and enjoyed working with. "I'd like to make the transfer to San Diego official. Work the cyber unit. Also a desk job so I can be there for David too. Train Farmer up some more. Given my age and years of service, I'll get to retire before Levi."

Julia scoffed. "Can you really tear yourself away from the computer, Nerd?"

Arm around Levi's shoulders, he squeezed him closer and made very public heart eyes at his husband. "The better question is, can I tear myself away from coming into work each day with this one?"

The groans and napkin baseballs were the hilarity he was after. As were Julia's smile and words. "Of course you can make the transfer official. And stay as long as you want to."

Levi shifted in his arms, angling to look at him again.

"What would you do if you retired? David's going to be out of the house by then, and I'll be at work all day."

He shrugged. "Always wanted to learn to surf."

More napkins sailed his direction.

"And on that note," Cam said as he stood, "I'm gonna go call my workaholic husband."

Matt rose beside him. "And I promised Gail I'd swing by tonight."

"She doing okay?" Levi asked.

"She's good," Matt said with a sly grin. Marsh didn't ask how that was going to work with him in LA. Granted it wasn't far between the two cities, but neither of their jobs were conducive to long distance.

"We need to go back to the office and check in on Catherine," Sutton said to Julia as they rose too. "I'll flag down the server for the check."

Marsh waved his hand. "We've got it."

"Fine, but don't stay too long," Julia said, splitting a look between them, "Big day tomorrow."

"Roger that, Eagle."

"What will you do all day?" Levi asked once the others were gone. "Besides surf?"

He lowered his voice and whispered in Levi's ear, "Whatever you need, baby." He dropped a kiss behind the lobe, then another on the hinge of Levi's jaw, loving the shiver that rippled through Levi's body against his. Loving the goose bumps that lifted on Levi's skin and tickled his lips where he trailed them down his neck. "Whatever will make you happy when you come home from work each day."

Using the hand still tangled with his, Levi laid them on Marsh's thigh, high enough to almost be indecent. His gravelly voice was over the line. "So you're going to be cooking naked in the kitchen every day?"

"Apron." He inched their hands higher and flicked his gaze to where his cock was starting to take notice. "To cover the sensitive bits."

Levi's splayed fingers ventured into indecent territory, his middle finger tracing the ridge of his erection. "Wouldn't want to hurt those."

"Levi."

"Maybe you'd like to go make out in the parking lot like we both wanted to our first night here."

"Fuck," Marsh groaned. "I wanted you so badly that night." He nipped the damn earlobe he couldn't get enough of. "Want you now."

"All you have to do is ask," Levi said, repeating Marsh's own words back to him from that night. "Ask, baby, and I'll give you what you need."

"Check!" Marsh practically shouted at the passing server while Levi grabbed his cowboy hat for him.

They laughed all the way to the car. Laughter Marsh swallowed when he shoved Levi up against the car door and claimed his mouth, claimed everything love and life had to promise, all of it wrapped up in the beautiful man in his arms.

"I wanted you that night too." Levi panted as Marsh kissed a trail down his throat. "Wanted a kiss and more."

Marsh popped open a shirt button so he could get at the base of Levi's neck, licking into the sensitive divot. "What else did you want?"

Levi grabbed an ass cheek and hauled him closer, their erections rutting together, their suit pants and boxers thin enough to feel the building heat between them. "Wanted you to manhandle me. Wanted you to take me home, fuck me good and hard, then hold me all night."

Marsh reached around him for the door handle. "In the car, now, before you get us arrested and we can't run the op tomorrow."

Levi feigned surprise with such a David-like "Me!" that Marsh laughed out loud. But then real surprise flitted over Levi's face when Marsh's phone rang. Marsh stepped back far enough to dig his phone out of his pocket. Wagner's name lit up the screen. "This hour for them," Levi said, "that can't be good."

Levi wasn't wrong. Marsh stepped the rest of the way out of his arms and answered the call, phone to his ear. "Wags, give me and Levi two seconds to get in the car." He grabbed his hat off the roof where it had fallen from Levi's head, circled the front of the RX, and slid into the passenger seat, Levi locking the doors as soon as Marsh shut his. Marsh tossed his hat in the back and flipped the phone to speaker. "What've you got?"

"I'm here with Ross and Binny." The other two agents said their hellos, and by the tone of each, Marsh already knew the news wasn't good. His and Levi's night was now headed in a different direction than it had been moments ago. "We've got movement on Sinclair, Catherine's contact from the train."

"According to Ajay," Binny said, "they've set up a half dozen NFT trading accounts over the weekend."

"Expecting an influx of currency," Levi surmised.

"They've also reached out to their Balkan contacts in Vienna," Ross said. "Let them know a shipment of cocaine is incoming from Mexico."

"We've got the op on our end here tomorrow," Marsh

told them. "But there's not actually supposed to be anyone on scene from the cartel. The weapons are supposed to go from Bratva hands into the Bureau's."

"Someone," Levi said—translation: Catherine—"made other plans."

"Catherine," Marsh said for the benefit of their colleagues on the other end of the line. "Anything else?"

"We're still digging," Binny said. "If we get an ID on the cartel contact, we'll let you know."

"Thank you, and good work," Marsh said before ending the call. "We have to call the team back in."

Beside him, Levi closed his eyes and rested his head back. "Fuck, I knew it after last night. I knew she was up to something. She can't let it go."

"You were right." Marsh laid a hand on his thigh. "You know her better than any of us. Do we go to her now or just let it play out?"

"Why would she help us? What does she gain by cooperating?" He shook his head. "Nothing. Worst-case scenario is in play."

Marsh inhaled, forcing back any panic, convincing himself there was no reason for it. "We're ready." He squeezed Levi's thigh, needing to convince him too. "Our team is ready. We've got this. This ends for Eder Capital tomorrow."

TWENTY-FOUR

THE TEAM HAD BACKED their play not to question Catherine again. She had zero incentive to cooperate at this point. There'd be no way to know if she was lying or telling the truth, and they didn't have time to waste figuring it out. They'd gotten what they were going to out of her, and with the additional information Marsh's legat team had supplied over the past twenty-four hours, they had a short list of likely cartel contacts who might be on the scene later. In any event, whatever information Catherine could have given them—and likely wouldn't have—also wouldn't fundamentally change the operation.

Which was in progress, and so far, all quiet. This time of early morning, there was very little traffic in this industrial area of Poway, a suburb northeast of San Diego proper, a short seven minutes from Levi's neighborhood. An occasional car would speed down Community, cutting from one residential side of town to the other, but that had dwindled to only one in the past ninety minutes.

"Delta, Echo, Foxtrot, report" Levi said.

Julia, Sutton, and Charlie each radioed "Clear" over the comms from their respective locations in parking lots near the choke points Levi and Marsh had previously identified.

In addition to the three perimeter teams, there were also three teams in the immediate vicinity of the Hagan Transport facility.

"Charlie team, report," Levi prompted.

"All clear from up here," Matt replied. He and his team had a south-side view of the building from across the street and up a steep embankment.

"Bravo team, report."

"Clear," Cam radioed from his team's position across the street to the east, fanned out among the sports fields of the local park, using the fence protectors for cover.

"Alpha team, clear," Levi finished from his and Marsh's team's position on the roof of a warehouse building directly behind the Hagan facility, overlooking the loading docks and parking lot.

Beside him, Marsh checked the tracking app on his comms tablet. "Transport is twenty minutes out." As if on cue, the door on the shortest of the four loading-dock bays began to slowly roll up. "Looks like the lone stranger inside got the same message."

Levi lifted hi-res, night-vision goggles to his eyes. "Bay door opening," he reported to the teams. He spotted legs inside and to the right of the door. "One individual. Control, be prepared for facial recognition in three, two, one." He clicked and held down the photo capture button on the goggles, hoping he snapped and transmitted enough pictures for Farmer to get an ID in the ten or so seconds before the person climbed down the metal loading-dock ladder and into the single remaining car in the lot.

"White male, midthirties, approximately five nine, two hundred twenty pounds," Farmer said. "Bulldog and Semper Fi tattooed on his shoulder. Jar—"

"Jarhead," Marsh and Julia said before Farmer finished getting the word out.

The cyber agent chuckled. "Should help narrow down the facial recognition. Search is running."

It took a short five minutes to identify the person still in the parking lot, waiting in his car, as a Hagan employee. No record; he was clean. Probably just following his boss's orders for some extra cash. Ten long minutes later, the transport finally arrived. The driver parked the cargo van at the open dock, climbed out, and without so much as a backward glance, hopped into the car with the other employee. A blink later, they were gone, the van left unguarded.

"What are you reading for security?" Levi asked Marsh.

"Nothing. Whatever they have, it's turned off."

"They don't want anyone to see," Cam said.

Marsh's tablet vibrated with an incoming text from Hawes. He read the message aloud to the rest of the team. "Birds of Prey"—Remy, Victoria, and Avery—"are two minutes out. Black X5. Traveling south on Community."

"Charlie team," Levi said. "That's you."

"We're monitoring," Matt confirmed.

"Alpha team," Cam radioed, "we've got party crashers behind you. Late model sedan, blackout windows, no lights on, riding low, especially the trunk." Which likely meant at least four people inside plus gear. "Creeping your direction down Stowe. Fifty yards."

Levi gestured for Alyssa and Will to take another member of their six-person team to the other side of the roof to cover their flank.

"X5 spotted," Matt radioed.

"Party crashers are stopped," Cam reported. "Thirty-five yards."

"We're clearly not the only ones with eyes on," Marsh said. "Everyone stay sharp."

The X5 swung into the parking lot and backed into a spot across from the van. Remy and Victoria climbed out of the passenger side of the SUV. "Canary and Oracle on the move. Huntress"—Avery—"still in the car."

"Makes sense," Marsh said. "She's the best driver of the three."

Remy and Victoria walked alongside the cargo van, phone flashlights on, inspecting inside the cab and under the body of the vehicle. Two professionals at work. Detecting nothing out of the ordinary, they climbed the metal steps onto the dock. A moment later, static crackled through the comms, then two *snap*s. Two *ping*s back from Farmer's end. The bug in the bay was set. Video on Marsh's tablet materialized a moment later. It was dark in the dock bay, but there was enough moonlight to see Remy and Victoria and the back of the cargo van, it's fender just below the lip of the short loading dock.

"Benz just turned onto Stowe from SPP," Julia radioed.

"Penguin," Farmer said, referring to Charles. "That's the car he left the Riddler's"—Anthony's—"place in."

Right on time. "Get the roadblocks in place," Levi told the perimeter teams before asking Cam for status.

"Party crashers still at thirty-five yards."

Levi flicked off his comm. "They had a window to steal the truck. They didn't take it. Could Catherine still be angling to kill her uncle?"

"You said it yourself. Discreet goes out the window with

her. They could also be with Charles. Either way, looks like they're waiting until after to rip off the shipment."

"From the Bratva? How does that make any sense if Catherine or Charles wanted to reopen those lines?"

"It doesn't. So they either know we're on them or they don't care."

"Fuck." Levi flipped his comm back on. "Everyone on your toes. This could get ugly."

"Are we sure the facility is empty?" Marsh queried.

"We tracked departures," Cam said. "All accounted for now that the last one left."

"Confirmed," Farmer said. "Drone detected no other heat signatures inside."

The Benz pulled into the lot.

"Party crashers on the move," Cam said. "Twenty-five yards. And stopped again."

"How—" Levi started as Charles slammed the car door. The *car*. "Check the Benz for signals."

"Already on it," Marsh said as he worked the tablet.

Meanwhile, through the loading-dock bug, Remy was squaring off with Charles. The picture was grainy and dim but good enough for evidence purposes. And the audio loud and clear. "A little warning would have been nice," she said. "You're lucky I didn't shoot you."

"Why didn't you?" Charles asked, the same skeptical tone he'd greeted Hawes with at the party Tuesday. He clearly wasn't in the habit of taking things at face value.

"Catherine warned me it could be a possibility."

Especially his niece. "The fed turned on her. Like I warned."

Remy took two steps back, both hands raised. "Maybe we should just call this whole thing off, then."

"If that's what you want." He gestured at the cargo van. "I'm happy to take these off your hands."

"The party crashers are his," Levi surmised.

Marsh nodded. "Maybe Catherine was wrong about her uncle's desire to reestablish lines with the Bratva. Or he just wanted to stick it to her as much as she did to him."

"Either way," Julia said, "we're prepared."

So was Remy for such an argument. "They're not yours to take. You're just the trafficker."

"And you, my dear," Charles said with a sneer, "are just a gunrunner. I fail to see the difference."

"I'm happy to call my boss if you need him to explain exactly what I am to him."

Matt whistled low over the comm. "The juice."

He wasn't wrong. And Charles was smart enough to recognize it too, backing down. "That won't be necessary."

"Good. Any trouble on the road?"

"None reported."

"I'd like to take a look," Remy said with a jut of her chin at the cargo van. "Make sure it's all still there."

"Of course." Charles turned to the cargo van doors and punched in the code on the electronic lock. He opened the van doors for Remy. Victoria hung back, keeping a watchful eye on Charles while Remy stepped off the ledge of the dock and into the van beside the stacks of wooden crates branded with winery logos. If they had been stopped on the road, the cargo would have just looked like a cellar transport from one California city to another. Remy withdrew a utility knife from her pocket and quickly opened the lid on the top crate. The row of bottles was expected, each secured in a notched wooden groove. Remy removed the bottles one by one, then the piece of particle board separating the layers. There was no more wine in the crate, only assault rifles, illegal, high-capacity magazines, and ammunition nestled among straw and what looked like bags of prescription drugs. Something the cartel would use on the other end to cut their drugs with. Or something that could be used to bribe the border guards with if they gave them any trouble.

"We got it," Farmer said over the comm.

Remy couldn't hear them, but she too was satisfied well enough with what she saw. She replaced the board, bottles, and lid, then climbed out of the truck, back onto the dock. "Very good." She closed the van doors and withdrew her phone. "I have the funds ready to transfer. Deposit back to you plus the shipping fee. I just need the account number from you."

Charles withdrew his own phone and rattled off one of the account numbers Farmer had fed to Catherine. A moment later, Charles nodded. "Received."

"Same," Farmer said.

Remy pocketed her phone. "We'll be in touch when the return shipment is ready for pick up."

"Very good. Please give Dimitri my regards," Charles said. "I miss working with him."

The hairs on the back of Levi's neck rose. Just how well did Charles know Dimitri? Well enough to check on the legitimacy of this transport? To learn it wasn't real?

If Remy was nervous about it, she didn't let it show. She extended a hand to Charles. "This should lead to more work." Then tilted her head toward the van. "Keys are in the cab?"

Charles nodded. "I'll close up here."

Remy and Victoria descended the metal stairs and

climbed into the van, the latter behind the wheel, Remy in the passenger seat.

"Too easy," Marsh muttered.

"Way too easy," Matt echoed.

Levi concurred, the hairs on his arms standing on end now too. "Bravo team, report."

"Party crashers still in place."

Avery cranked the X5 and pulled out of the lot first. Victoria cranked the cargo van, and Levi couldn't lie and say he didn't hold his breath, releasing it only when an explosion didn't follow. She pulled the van away from the dock and turned toward the exit.

Levi glanced back at Charles, who was closely watching the departing van, who, as it crossed in front of the Benz tapped his phone, then slammed shut the cargo bay door.

The *car*.

"Everyone get down!" Levi shouted, not bothering to keep his voice low. He threw himself over Marsh just as an explosion lit the night sky, blinding in its intensity, thunderous in the force of the blast, vibrations rocking the nearby buildings, deafening Levi's hearing, and heaving a wave of heat, smoke, and debris in all directions, driving Levi, Marsh, and their team back from the edge of the building they were hiding on.

But even through the smoky haze and the ringing in his ears, Levi heard and felt the second explosion, witnessed the fresh flare of red, orange, and yellow painting the night sky through the clouds of smoke filling it.

The cargo van.

Oh, Hawes Madigan was going to be pissed.

"Levi! Babe!" Two hands framing his face. Brown eyes staring into his. His husband. "Are you okay?" Marsh's voice sounded distant like he was shouting from miles away, not mere inches. "Levi, baby, answer me!"

"I'm fine." He shook his head, dislodging Marsh's hold and the blast disequilibrium that had momentarily unbalanced him. "Are you? The team?"

"I'm fine. We're all fine here. But we need to go!"

Tires squealed from the direction of the road.

Levi found his legs and dashed back to the edge of the building, peering through the smoke. Avery swung the X5 around in the street, leaving it parked at the lot exit, a barricade, as she threw open the door and charged toward the burning van.

"Party crashers on the move," Cam radioed.

Levi pressed a hand to his ear, confirming the comm device was still firmly in place. "Bravo team, converge on the party crashers. Charlie team, converge and cover the building exits. The Penguin is in there somewhere. Alpha team converging for recovery."

One last glance down—Avery dragging a body from the cab—and then Levi was running for the fire escape the rest of his team was descending.

"Delta, Echo, Foxtrot, converge on the target facility," Marsh said as they hit the ground. "Backup needed. No one's bugging out of this one."

That was one way to put it. And the right call. Levi clasped his shoulder in thanks, and then they were running again. Levi kept one eye on the burning van and the other on the sedan spinning out in the intersection ahead, surrounded by Cam's team. The doors were flung open and four people spilled out, shots firing.

Levi gestured Will, Alyssa, and one of their other agents ahead. "Provide cover."

They nodded and charged ahead while Levi, Marsh, and two others on their team slid through the narrow space in front of the X5. "Friendlies!" Marsh shouted, before pulling his windbreaker up over his mouth and nose.

The smoke was thick, making Levi's eyes sting and his lungs hurt. But they pressed toward the heat that rippled over his skin like searing waves. "Avery!" Levi hollered, giving up the pretext, their cover no longer necessary. "Where are you?"

"Here!" she yelled between racking coughs that did not sound good.

They raced toward her voice, found her ten or so feet from the burning van, dragging an unconscious Remy next to where Victoria was already laid out on the ground.

"Get Vic," Marsh called as he rushed to Avery's side, holding her up with one arm while hefting Remy's frighteningly lifeless body over his shoulder, the formerly pale skin of her arms already mottled with burns.

Oh, the Bratva captain was going to be pissed.

Levi moved to one side of Victoria, the other agent with them on her other side. They hauled her up between them, a cough and groan from her still mostly Gumby form welcome noise to Levi's ears. "We've got you. Just hang on."

They hustled away from the van and away from the firefight on the street to a dumpster enclosure at the back corner of the lot. "Shut the gate behind us," Levi ordered the other agent. "And keep watch." He leaned Victoria up against the brick corner. "Check her over," he said to Avery, then scooted next to where Marsh had laid Remy out on the ground and had started CPR. He moved next to her head. "I've got this," he told Marsh. "You take chest compressions." They worked together, all the while keeping an ear on the action in the street, all the while worrying that Remy only seemed to get colder to the touch, her body still frighteningly still but for the breaths he was blowing into her lungs.

He glanced at Marsh, who shot the same *we're fucked* glance back at him.

Sudden movement from Avery drew Levi's gaze aside. She was pointing at Remy's hand. "Her fingers just moved."

His gaze shot back to Remy. He didn't see it. He leaned down, feeling for breath against his face because he sure as fuck wouldn't hear anything faint over the ringing in his ears.

One beat, two beats, and then he felt it. "I've got breaths."

Marsh grasped her wrist and closed his eyes. Opened them a second later with a nod. "Got a pulse. Weak but there."

"I'm gonna call in support," Levi said as he shuffled back over to Avery and the other agent. He crouched beside them. "Will you be good here?"

Avery flipped a knife over in her hand. "We're good."

The agent likewise nodded.

Marsh stood beside them, offering Levi a hand up. He didn't let go once Levi was standing. "Are you okay?" he asked. "Breathing? Burns?"

"I'm good." Levi squeezed his hand. "You?" Marsh nodded. "All right, then, let's go catch the Penguin once and for all."

TWENTY-FIVE

CAM WAS LEADING point on the party crashers, assisted by Charlie and her team who had arrived on scene, the two forces swiftly neutralizing the unknown entities. Two dead, one in cuffs, the other fleeing on foot onto the Poway Trail. Julia was leading her team after the runner. She was an avid hiker. Probably knew that trail backward and forward. Never mind she was an excellent tracker. Marsh had no doubt she'd catch them.

Sutton's team had also arrived on scene and surrounded the building, freeing up Matt and his team to enter the building and join Marsh and Levi in the hunt for Charles Sanders.

"ETA on the drone?" Marsh queried Farmer.

"Drone is there," Farmer replied. "Can't get a read on heat signatures for the smoke and flames."

"Fucking hell."

"So we do this the old-fashioned way," Levi said from the other side of the door where they were crouched, still in the shadow of the loading docks, the main bullpen area across the threshold. "Matt, anything? Any sightings up front?"

"Negative," Matt said. "We're fanned out across the lobby. No sign of him here or on cursory glance, in the bullpen."

"Marsh and I are at the back. Grid inspection. Check every office and cubicle. Meet in the middle."

"Roger that."

Marsh glanced across at Levi, held his gaze a long moment, then with a nod, they began to systematically work the back rows of the bullpen. Checking each desk and cubicle, each office on either end of the rows, until they met Matt's team in the middle of the cavernous space.

"He's not on this level," Marsh said.

"We're sure he didn't slip out?" Levi asked Matt.

"Not that we saw. You said he ran into the building. Visual confirmed that." He held up his phone, the feed from Levi's own goggles before the explosion. "He didn't come out any other point."

Levi nodded. "Charlie, any movement from the building outside?"

"Negative," she replied.

"Upstairs it is, then," Marsh said.

They filed into the stairwell, eight of them, Marsh in the lead. He was reaching for the second-floor door when Levi's, "Hold," echoed up the line. Everyone stilled, no sound, no movement.

Except the *click* of the roof door latch a floor up.

Levi pointed up, then at the door where Marsh had his grip on the handle, mouthing the words, "Fake it."

Marsh nodded and opened the door. He held it open as Levi moved to the front and led the line of agents up the last flight of stairs to the roof door. Marsh let the second-floor door close and fell into position at the back of the line. He gave Levi another nod.

Levi tested the roof door. Unlocked. He crouched low and pushed it open slowly. Marsh released the breath he'd been holding when no gunfire greeted them. Levi slipped out through the door, the other agents silently following and fanning out. Marsh was the last to exit and he closed the door just shy of fully, no click.

Charles was nowhere immediately in sight. Levi signaled for Matt and two agents to do a sweep around the stair enclosure. They made quick work of it. No sign of Charles in their immediate vicinity. Which meant he was somewhere among or behind the line of HVAC units ahead of them. He flashed Levi six fingers, then two, then three, reminding him and the team of the setup. Six units, two rows, three units each.

"Three lines," Marsh mouthed silently, then pointed at the three paths, to the left of the units, between them, to the right.

Levi and Matt nodded, and the rest of the agents divided and lined up behind them. They started a slow walk toward the other side of the building, carefully checking in and around each unit. Halfway there, Charles darted out from behind the second-to-last unit, into the middle aisle, fifteen feet in front of Marsh. And fired.

"Get down!" Marsh crouched, the bullet that whizzed past barely missing him, thankfully missing the agents behind him who'd immediately heeded his warning. "Suspect armed!"

No use keeping quiet as Charles clearly knew they were there. What he didn't know was the coverage they had on both other sides. He hung left, Levi's direction, and the ensuing gunfire sent Marsh's pulse rocketing into his throat. "Put down your weapon!" Levi called.

"Converge!" Marsh whisper-shouted his order, and Matt's team materialized through the units, joining Marsh's, and together, they funneled through to back up Levi's. Matt and Marsh darted ahead instead, coming around the back of where Charles had slipped through to Levi's lane.

Marsh quickly assessed the scene. Two agents down, Levi and Charles in a standoff, their weapons trained on each other. Marsh leveled his at the back of Charles's head, Matt beside him doing the same.

Levi's gaze stayed locked on Charles, not giving away Marsh and Matt. "You're outnumbered Charles. Put down your weapon and surrender. We can make this go easier on you."

Charles didn't budge. "I won't become your pawn like my niece."

"We're not asking you to," Levi said. "You control your own destiny here. Your play."

"My plays were apparently not as well planned as they'd seemed."

"The party crashers weren't yours?" Levi asked as Marsh and Matt inched closer. "Or the bomb in the Benz?" He was almost within arm's reach. "Let us take you in. Protective custody."

Charles scoffed. "You don't know what those words mean."

"It means we'll do everything we can to keep you alive."

"What if I don't want to be?" Charles yanked up his

gun, pointing it at his own head instead. "I won't be anyone's pawn."

Marsh and Matt lunged, the latter at Charles's body, arms wrapped around his middle, pulling him backward, while Marsh ripped the gun from his hand the opposite direction. "Checkmate, motherfucker."

Except they weren't the only players on the board.

The bullet came out of nowhere, and in the blink of an eye, Charles Sanders's brain was splattered everywhere.

TWENTY-SIX

HAIR DAMP, shirt collar unbuttoned, tie hanging loose around his neck, Levi entered the Bureau break room and found several of his team similarly trying to pull themselves back together after a too-long, too-eventful night and early morning. Marsh sat at one of the round tables dressed in jeans and a Bureau T-shirt, hands cupped around a steaming mug of coffee. Farmer sat beside him, laptop open, scrolling through what looked like rap sheets for the two party crashers in custody. Alyssa stood by the window with her own cup of joe, and Matt stood in front of the open fridge, staring inside but a million miles away. More likely twenty or so miles to the east, where a bullet a few inches to the left would have left him dead instead of Charles Sanders.

A few inches the other direction and it could have been Marsh. Levi suppressed the shiver that threatened. He'd have to process that later; Matt needed him now.

He crossed the room, coasting a hand over Marsh's shoulders as he passed behind him, needing that reassurance, that confirmation he was safe and sound. The shivers backed off, and he made his way to Matt. He gently pried the fridge door from the other agent's grip, pushed it closed, then looped an arm around Matt's shoulders. When he didn't resist, Levi drew him the rest of the way into a hug. "Close calls suck."

Matt inhaled a shuddery breath as he returned the embrace and returned to the here and now. "Every time."

"When we become numb to them, that's when there's a problem." Levi drew back. "You got the number for the employee assistance counselor?"

Matt nodded. "Appointment later today, and don't you ever say again that you wouldn't make a good ASAC." He squeezed his shoulder, then opened the fridge again, this time with purpose, retrieving the half gallon of milk. "You want any of this for your tea?"

Levi shook his head. "Not a London fog kind of morning." He liked black tea occasionally when he needed a stiffer shot of caffeine, but this morning—he glanced at the wall clock, nearly afternoon—he needed calm.

Marsh had apparently sensed that already. "Two peppermint tea bags in the mug by the coffeemaker."

Levi spotted the cup and smiled despite the hell of the past however many hours they'd been awake. A simple gesture that saved his teetering sanity. He filled the mug with hot water and slid into the seat beside Marsh. "Thank you."

"Welcome," Marsh said with a kiss to his temple. "And Matt's right. You'll make a terrific ASAC."

He opened his mouth to protest the accuracy and inevitability of that statement but was cut short by Marsh's phone vibrating on the table. A notification flashed on-screen—a text from Julia.

Today was a day Levi was happy not to have the ASAC title. Julia, Cam, and Sutton had taken point coordinating last night's operation with local authorities. SDPD and the sheriff's department had been notified in advance and had deferred to the Bureau, but once two giant fireballs had lit up the night sky, all bets were off. The SACs and ASACs had had to stay on scene after Levi, Marsh, Matt, and the rest of the team had given their statements and left at sunrise. Now, five plus hours later, Julia and Cam were downtown at SDPD headquarters while Sutton and Charlie were meeting with the federal prosecutor in advance of Catherine's arraignment this afternoon. No one had slept, no one had gone home, and Julia's message, which Marsh opened and displayed on-screen, didn't give Levi much hope for either of those things anytime soon.

Anthony press conference. 12:15. Shelter.

Marsh cursed, and Matt leaned over his shoulder to read the message. "Are you fucking kidding me? He's doing that? Today? Does he want to be shot too?"

"I don't think he's worried about getting shot," Marsh replied, then said to Farmer, "Go back through everything we have on Anthony and all his accounts. Look for any unusual activity, anything that connects him to the party crashers or to anyone that's been arrested for explosives-related crimes."

"Sharpshooters too?" Farmer asked.

"Yes," Marsh said with a nod. "To the extent we have anything that can connect those dots. Then cross-reference against all leads on Greg and Amanda."

Levi followed, even if it made his stomach sink. "You think Anthony arranged the hit?"

"The hit and/or the explosion. That Benz was at Anthony's house. It was rigged."

"By Charles, to blow up the weapons and the deal."

"That's what we thought at the time, and maybe that's the case, but what if that's not what Charles was doing on his phone right before the explosion."

"I'll reach out to evidence," Matt said, heading for the door. "Expedite the processing of the activity log from the phone."

"Alyssa," Marsh said, "let's get a status check on Blaine too." She nodded and followed Matt out the door.

Levi took a sip of his tea and gathered his thoughts, trying to put last night and this new theory into context with everything they knew. "This isn't the plan Stefan told you."

"The plan *Stefan* knew," Marsh said. "But plans change all the time. Catherine told Charles to cut his losses. What if Anthony decided to do the same? He'd gotten what he could out of the Sanderses, same as he had out of Greg and Amanda. Too much of a liability now. So he sent a killer after them."

"But aren't they like father and son?" Farmer said. "Would they really turn on each other that way?"

"The board can't have two kings," Marsh replied.

Kings. Another thought occurred to Levi, but he needed to approach it delicately.

"Farmer, can you give us the room for a minute?"

"No problem." He pushed to his feet, taking his laptop with him. "This will go faster if I'm directly wired."

While he gathered his things, Levi stood and snagged

the remote from the wall beside the TV, where it was stuck with a piece of Velcro. He flipped to one of the local news channels, muted it for the time being, then closed the door on his way back to the table. His ass had barely hit the seat when Marsh correctly surmised where his mind had gone.

"You want to know if it could've been the Madigans?"

"Hawes's feed went out the other night at the party, and Avery disappeared from the scene with Remy and Victoria before EMS arrived."

"If not for the guns, they'd be at the top of my suspect list too." Levi's surprise must have shown on his face because Marsh chuckled. "You never noticed their absence when you were with them?"

Now that Levi thought about it, there hadn't been any in the car safe Hawes had accessed that day. None around the house, MCS, or on any of their persons. "I didn't think about it then," he admitted. "And if I had, I would have assumed they were locked up because of the kids."

"No," Marsh said. "They're not there at all. Long story, but it ended with a firm no-guns policy."

"Huh." He sat back in his chair and raked a hand through his hair. "So not the Madigans. Probably not the Bratva either."

"You see how I got to Anthony."

"I do," he said with a nod. "But we need to eliminate another possibility first. Catherine."

TWENTY-SEVEN

LEVI NAVIGATED the RX through every shortcut to downtown his thirty-eight years in San Diego had taught him. All the while, Anthony's press conference played from Marsh's phone on the dash. Levi's resulting rage drove his speed higher, shaving minutes off their drive time to the federal courthouse.

The congressman spoke of Greg's and Amanda's dedication to the shelter, to helping women and children to safety and a second chance, to his commitment to continue funding the shelter and their search for a new assistant director and programs manager. Notably, he was on the sidewalk in front of the shelter, clearly unconcerned about his safety. Another point for Marsh's theory of the case.

He invited questions about the shelter, about Greg's and Amanda's legacies—Levi rolled his eyes—and of course about his efforts to support such causes, but the gathered press had already moved on to the latest scandal swirling around the congressman.

"Representative Anthony," one of the reporters called, "any comment on reports that your close friend and host of Tuesday night's donor event, Charles Sanders, died in an FBI sting last night?"

Anthony had the good sense not to pull the same *I had no idea act* he had when news broke of Greg's and Amanda's deaths. That said, his, "Reports are unconfirmed," reply was even less convincing and invited a barrage of follow-up questions.

"Is Charles Sanders alive?"

"Did you know he was a suspected trafficker?"

"Did he use illegal channels to donate to your last campaign?"

"Did you know it was dirty money?"

"What happened in Salzburg last week?"

Anthony coughed, that last question catching him off guard. "We're not here to discuss this today. We're here to honor Greg and Amanda and their contributions to the shelter."

"Are their deaths connected?" the first reporter asked. "Is the shelter a front?"

"Give that one a gold star!" Marsh said.

It was also apparently the straw that broke Anthony's civility mask. "Again, I'm not here to discuss Charles or whatever may have happened last night," he snapped. "But I will say this. If my dear friend Charles was killed as part of some unfounded, botched FBI raid, we need oversight, and we need it now. Greg and Amanda, Charles, where does the incompetence end? How many lives is a vindictive agent's personal vendetta going to cost?"

"What agent? What vendetta?"

Anthony left the podium without taking further questions. He handed his mic to his press secretary and climbed into an SUV that screeched away from the curb.

Just as Levi was screeching into the federal building parking lot. He swung the RX into a spot and threw it in park. But prying his hand from where he was white-knuckling the wheel proved a challenge. "We have to tie this up. We have to nail him ASAP." He wanted this to be fucking over, wanted his life back, wanted the bad guys behind bars and a future with the man beside him. The future the rings on their fingers promised.

Marsh laid a hand on his thigh. "We will, babe. We're close, or he wouldn't be making desperate moves. Making sacrifices left and right."

"He's laying all the blame at the Bureau's feet."

"Buzzwords," Marsh said. "All the right ones to rile up his base. But he won't get away with it this time." He reached across Levi's body and covered his hand, gently prying his fingers from the wheel, then holding his hand in his. "We won't let him."

Levi closed his eyes and leaned back in his seat, channeling all the boiling anger that had simmered for too long into the fist he curled inside Marsh's big hands, letting him absorb and dissipate the fury with soft sweeps of his thumbs. When his fist finally relaxed, Levi opened his eyes and met the brown ones watching him. "Thank you."

Marsh wove their fingers together. "I'm amazed you held it together as long as you did."

He inhaled deep once more, recentering. "Okay, how do we want to play this?"

"Don't let on to our theory about Anthony. Not right

away. See where she leads you, but from there, it's your call. You've read her right from the go."

"Except I read last night wrong." He started to close his eyes again, frustration welling up, but Marsh gave his hand a squeeze, drawing his attention back.

"We don't know that yet. Maybe she was involved. At a minimum, she set some of that in motion. We need to assess how much. What's been Catherine's priority all along?"

Easiest question of the day, hell, the past five weeks. "Catherine."

"Right, so play to that. Did killing her uncle put her in a better or worse position? And how do we use that self-interest to our benefit to nail Anthony because we also set some part of this in motion."

Levi debated different lines of questioning the entire way to the holding room. Where to start? How to lead Catherine to the answers they needed? But when Catherine stepped through the door, the glint of victory in her eyes told him everything he needed to know about where to start. She'd heard the news about Charles and was happy with the outcome. Question was, had she engineered it? "Did you miss me, Agent Bishop?"

Since she knew Charles was dead, there was no sense beating around the bush. "Did you have your uncle killed?"

She adjusted the collar on the suit coat she'd donned for her arraignment. "I have no idea what you're talking about. He texted me last night. Last I heard from him."

He banged the table with a palm. "Dammit, Catherine."

Fiddled with the sleeves. "How's dear Stewart handling the death of his so-called father?"

He sensed she was fishing. For the fallout from her actions? Or to navigate going forward? Levi gave her a little info, hoping for some in return. "He's disclaiming any knowledge. Laying it all at the FBI's feet."

She shrugged and slumped back in her chair, crossing one leg over the other. "Why do you think it was me and not him? Why should I keep involving myself in this? Why can't I just sit here, let you do your jobs, let Stewart implode, and claim the spoils of war?"

There was the directional sign he needed. "You could help us get there faster. Help us nail Anthony and help yourself."

"I've helped you enough."

"We were going to use Charles to leverage Anthony. Charles is off the board now. We have to get Anthony another way."

"And how am I supposed to help you do that?"

"Give us Blaine."

"His son?" She laughed out loud. "His fucking accomplice," she hissed lower. "What good will that do?"

"Because if he's willing to kill his so-called father, what makes any of us think he won't kill his own son? Or you?"

She hesitated, and Levi leaned harder into her self-interest, into any human's instinct for self-preservation. "If you didn't kill Charles last night, Blaine is your best chance for clearing your name and pinning it on Anthony, and you need to, Catherine, if you want to stay alive. It's not only Anthony's hit list you're on now."

She stiffened, and her gaze sharpened on him, seeming to finally sense the razor-thin edge she was tap dancing on. "What do you mean?"

"It's not a far stretch for Dimitri Petrov to think the person who killed Charles Sanders also killed his favorite." The second lie he'd told in all this.

Catherine inhaled a sharp breath as her eyes grew wide as saucers. "Remy's dead?"

"Along with one of Hawes's captains." And the third. "Surely you want Petrov and Madigan to know it wasn't you."

She bought it, going pale as a ghost. "I'll make the call."

TWENTY-EIGHT

BY THE TIME Catherine's arraignment was over that afternoon, she had arranged a meet with Blaine Anthony. Four o'clock at a yakitori place in Clairemont. The location was consistent with Levi's team's work tracking down Representative Anthony's son. Farmer had continued to analyze the surveillance footage from Sunday in Temecula, and while he couldn't get a usable shot of the tags or VIN of the SUV Blaine had jumped into, he had managed to get a relatively clean shot of an oil change sticker on the front windshield for a drive-thru service station off Clairemont Mesa Boulevard. A visit from Alyssa and Will later, and the team had identified the owner of the SUV, a grad student who rented an apartment in Clairemont. After a visit with him, they'd learned he was a former classmate of Blaine's. And an occasional fuck buddy. Blaine would sometimes couch surf at his apartment and would usually wander into his bed. A fact that made Blaine's life, Marsh figured, even more disposable to his father. According to Blaine's friend, Anthony knew Blaine was gay and forced him to stay in the closet with blackmail and emotional manipulation over Blaine's supposed role in his mother's death some years back. Marsh also figured Blaine had zero to do with that, but when your dad had the kind of power Anthony did, the kind of friends who trafficked guns, girls, and more and used you to help them, Blaine probably couldn't see a way clear of the mess he'd let his father suck him into. Until now.

"I'm sure he wants out from under his father's thumb more than anyone," Marsh said as he and Levi crossed the street. Blaine had entered ten minutes ago. They'd remained in the RX, parked at the curb across the street, making sure no one followed Blaine inside or set up camp in the parking lot.

"Why hasn't he run, then?" Levi asked. "He's got the skills to forge the documents." He waved his own fake passport in the air. "Money stashed in accounts all over, according to Frederick. But he's still here."

"I doubt it's loyalty to his father."

"It can't be," Levi said. "Not after what we learned today."

They were halfway up the sidewalk to the restaurant when Marsh's phone vibrated, an incoming call from Sutton. He stepped off the walkway, out of anyone's way and out of anyone's earshot. Levi moved beside him, close enough to hear the phone Marsh held between them. "Sutton, we're at the restaurant," Marsh said. "About to meet with Blaine. What's up?"

"Catherine made bail."

Levi raked a hand through his hair. "Fuck, that was fast." Though not a surprise. They'd been warned by the federal prosecutor that Catherine's attorney had requested bail and used her cooperation with the FBI as reason to grant it. They'd also seized her passport. Little comfort as Marsh and Levi stood outside a restaurant preparing to meet her forger of choice. "Who paid it?" Levi asked.

"Stewart Anthony."

"Jesus Christ," Levi muttered. "There goes the distancing himself from the Sanderses theory." He started to stalk away, but Marsh looped an arm around his waist, drawing him back close. He was tired, angry, and at the end of his rope with this case; they all were. But they were close; Marsh could taste it.

"Yes and no," Sutton said. "He spun it to fit his narrative. Doing right by his surrogate family, he and Catherine together in their time of grief, the two of them against the Bureau." News had broken midafternoon that Charles Sanders was in fact dead. "But when pressed, Anthony made no comments on the charges against either of them."

"Did she leave the federal building with him?" Levi asked.

"No. She refused his offer. Asked to be taken back to the safehouse instead."

Levi leaned some of his weight against Marsh's side. "Thank fuck for that."

"Do we think she'll actually stay there?" Marsh said. "She's free to leave, correct?"

"She is," Sutton said. "But whatever you said to her, Levi, she's spooked. I don't think she's going anywhere."

Levi covered his face with his hands and sank more fully into Marsh, who made a swift exit from the call with Sutton. "What did you tell her?" he asked Levi after hanging up.

"That Remy and Victoria were dead and she needed Blaine to clear her name with the Bratva and Madigans."

Marsh whistled low as he rubbed a hand over his husband's hunched shoulders. "Bold move, Cotton." Levi elbowed his side, and Marsh chuckled. "And to think, I was going to tell you not to worry." He tilted his head toward the restaurant. "Let's go see if your move pays off."

The restaurant was tiny inside. The yakitori took up a good portion of the center of the space, a bar around it, no one behind the glass at the grill or at the hostess stand, the place still technically closed. A single row of two-person booths were against the wall to the left of the bar, the rest of the dining room was to the right, four-person booths along the edge of the space and a few four-tops in the middle. They didn't see Blaine at first, tucked as he was in the corner, the high booth dividers either direction blocking their view of him, the black of his hoodie blending in with the restaurant's interior. They only noticed him there when a person who Marsh guessed was one of the chefs came out of the back with a bottle of Sapporo and dropped it at his table.

They waited for the chef, who acknowledged their presence with a nod, to pass back through the curtains into the kitchen before approaching the booth. Blaine didn't startle, expecting them it seemed, casually drinking his beer and letting his hoodie fall back off his head. Catherine must have warned him it would be them and not her. Good sign that he still came, though Marsh wondered what else she'd told him. Marsh gestured for Levi to slide into the booth first, across from Blaine, who had his back to the wall, putting Marsh's and Levi's to the door. Marsh didn't like it, but if he was forced to sit this direction, he'd make his bigger body the target.

Because Blaine sure as fuck didn't look like he would be quick to move. Brown eyes bloodshot, beard overgrown and scruffy, the longer top strands of his dark hair greasy and drooping over the shaved underside, the black paint on his nails chipped and his cuticles destroyed, Blaine looked like a stressed-out mess.

Levi recognized it too. "Are you as tired as we are?"

A beleaguered laugh slipped out as Blaine finished his beer. "And you guys have only been dealing with this for a few years. Try twenty-five." He picked at the label on the bottle, not meeting their gazes, his shoulders slumped and the corners of his mouth turning impossibly lower. "Is Grandpa Charles really dead?"

Grandpa. Blaine wasn't just stressed out. He was grieving. Anthony clearly wasn't the only one who considered Charles family, though by the look and sound of Blaine, by the evidence pointing at Anthony, only Blaine actually knew what family meant.

"He is," Levi said, voice gentle, commiserating. Charles may have been evil, but that didn't negate the hole that was now left in Blaine's life. "I'm sorry for your loss."

Blaine inhaled deeply, slid the empty aside, and propped his elbows on the table, raking his hands through his hair. "Dad's unchecked, then."

A hole bigger than either of them understood. "Your dad?" Marsh said. "Not Charles?"

"Charles was always the better chess player. More careful. Strategic." He combed his hands though his hair once more, then left them clasped behind his neck. "Dad's a bully, plain and simple. Pretty sure Charles is the only reason I'm still alive. He gave me a role in all this. Made it so Dad couldn't kill me too."

Levi stiffened beside him. "Too?" he choked out. "Your mother?"

"In a manner of speaking."

Levi slumped back in the booth and hung his head. Granted, they'd already discussed the possibility that Blaine could be a target, that the circumstances surrounding Mrs. Anthony's death were suspicious, but that was Levi the investigator. *Hearing* it from Blaine, though, made it more real to Marsh and no doubt sent Levi, the husband and father, reeling.

While his partner struggled to recover, Marsh leaned forward and into the opening Blaine had given them. "We can give you a role too, Blaine, in taking back your life."

"But I don't know anything about what happened last night other than what I've seen on the news."

"Why don't we start from the beginning, and we'll see if that's really the case?"

"How far back do you want to go?"

"Let's start with the Sixth Avenue Shelter."

As Blaine detailed the countless forgeries he'd done for victims trafficked through the shelter, Levi worked his way back into the conversation, the investigator returning to the forefront. Asking who Blaine's primary point of contact was—Amanda, usually, Greg and Stefan sometimes. How he was paid—cash or bitcoin. If there had been forged papers for folks other than the victims—yes, and it was usually Catherine who made those requests. Until things had begun to go off the rails for Amanda. At first, she'd asked for new IDs for her, Johnny, and Frederick, but Blaine hadn't been able to turn those around as fast. It was quicker when she'd ask for hers and Greg's, the former already done.

"You were in Temecula last weekend to give her the IDs?" Marsh asked.

He nodded. "I was actually going to try to convince her to go to the feds with me. I knew Greg never would, he was too afraid of my dad, but she was like me, dragged into this mess by our parents."

"That wasn't the impression we got," Levi said. "She was all in."

"Yes, she drank the Kool-Aid, but I grew up with her. I believed there was some good in there still. And you guys had been good to Frederick. Kept him safe."

Marsh wasn't sure he shared Blaine's faith in his childhood friend, but that was neither here nor there at this point. Blaine had gone there to try to do right and stumbled onto something very wrong. "What did you see that night in Temecula?"

"It was dark, okay? So it's not like I can be as precise as when I'm doing a forgery."

"Just tell us what you can," Levi encouraged, then laid his phone on the table, the voice memo app open. "Is it okay if I record this?"

"In case my father kills me?"

"No, so I can play this back to our sketch artist and have them draw it digitally. Then we can run it through facial recognition."

"Sure, and I can also get them partway there." He shouted something in Japanese that Marsh didn't understand, but a moment later, the chef from before appeared with a paper menu, a pen, and another beer. "Thank you," Blaine told him, then began to describe the hitman as he drew him on the back of the menu between sips of beer. Even in the dark, Blaine had seen a lot, more than most people, his attention to detail better than average owing to his forgery activities.

"Is there anything else you remember about that night?" Levi asked once he'd finished the drawing.

"Yeah." He sat back, bottle in hand. "He called my dad and said it was done."

No power in the universe could have stopped Marsh from lurching forward. "You're sure?"

"I know that asshole's voice." He drained the rest of his beer, picked up the pencil to make a final adjustment to the suspect's nose, then pencil down again, spun the sketch and pushed it across the table to Marsh and Levi. "He's probably already gone by now."

"I'm not so sure," Levi said. "Charles was killed by a professional. Same as Greg and Amanda."

He tipped the beer bottle toward the sketch. "You think that's the guy?"

"Could be," Levi said.

"And if it is," Marsh continued, "then you actually did know a lot about what happened last night."

"If you get an ID on him, tell Frederick to check for transactions with Nathan White. It's the name my dad used for motels when he checked in with his mistresses." He rolled his eyes. "Made me draw up fake papers for him and everything."

While Levi scribbled the name on the menu, Marsh contemplated next steps. "We need to get you into protective custody."

"Unnecessary." Marsh whipped around in the booth, surprised by the familiar voice, unsurprised he'd been able to sneak up on him. For as tall and muscular as Hawes's husband was, he moved like a ghost. "We've got him," Chris said.

"Someone's already got another role for me," Blaine said. "Get my dad behind bars this weekend, and I'll go on record with whatever you need to make it stick." He slid out of the booth and grabbed his two bottles. "Until then, I'm taking my chances with Canadian Tuxedo."

TWENTY-NINE

WITH THE INFORMATION Blaine had supplied, it had been a fast and furious twenty hours as the team scrambled to ID the shooter, tie him and the party crashers to Anthony, and bring the rest of the case together. They'd worked in shifts, everyone getting a rotation at home for sleep, including Marsh and Levi, who'd spent a couple much-needed hours with family, then a few even more needed hours asleep in each other's arms. The sun was barely up when Marsh had left for the office and Levi for the safehouse to check on Catherine. Marsh had offered to go with him, but Levi had wanted to make the stop quick, which he had, arriving at the office less than an hour behind Marsh, Catherine safe and sound. By early afternoon, the entire team was reassembled in the war room to brief each other on progress and to see if they had enough to move on Anthony.

Farmer sat at the head of the table nearest the screen, one half displaying Blaine's sketch of Greg and Amanda's murderer. "Using Blaine's sketch plus the additional details he'd provided, facial recognition returned a match. Robert Black." Farmer clicked his mouse, and photos of Black's California ID and US passport filled the other half of the screen. "Thirty-three, brown hair and beard, blue eyes, relatively nondescript but for a scar right here." Farmer used the laser pointer on his phone to indicate the bare spot in their suspect's goatee near the right corner of his mouth. "He entered the US at the CBX Friday before last." He clicked his mouse again, and the pictures on-screen were replaced with a recorded video feed from the Tijuana Cross Border Terminal. Their suspect approached the pedestrian checkpoint dressed in sneakers, jeans, a concert tee, and carrying a backpack. One CBP officer scanned his passport and asked the purpose of his trip. He pointed to his T-shirt with a smile and told the officer about the show. Another officer ushered him through the metal detector, patted him down, and checked his backpack. All clear, they sent him on his way.

"Did he cross with anything else?" Cam asked.

"Nope," Farmer said. "Just what you see."

"Not unusual here," Julia explained. "Lots of daily foot traffic. Locals going back and forth and tourists who've figured out it's cheaper to fly to San Diego, walk across the border there"—she gestured at the screen—"then hop on a dirt-cheap in-country flight to get elsewhere in Mexico."

"Robert Black," Charlie said. "Sounds like an alias."

"Give that agent a prize!" Marsh said from where he sat across the table next to Levi. He nodded to Farmer, who put Blaine's sketch back on the screen next to a nearly identical photo of a man ten years younger. His brown hair was buzzed, his jaw was shaved clean, the scar clearly visible, and his USMC uniform was heavily decorated. "Corporal

Justin Heard," Marsh said. "USMC Scout Sniper. Rumor has it the scout snipers won't have their own platoon much longer. They're being wrapped into reconnaissance, which might explain why Heard didn't reenlist earlier this year."

"And he found other work," Sutton said. "Quickly."

On Marsh's other side, Alyssa opened a folder and pushed the top picture into the center of the table. "Because he'd crossed paths with Anthony before. He was loaned out for a protection detail last year. Guess who else was on that protection detail?" She slid another photo next to Heard's. "Your jarhead from Hagan Transport. Diego Morales."

"Which connects him to the other scene." Sutton made a victory fist but stopped short of banging the table with it. "It's still circumstantial."

"Wait for it," Levi teased, then gestured for Alyssa to continue.

"One of a couple possibilities here," she said with a gesture toward the photos. "Morales confirmed coordinates to Heard. Maybe sent him building plans. Or he just left the door open like his buddy asked."

"In any event," Julia said, "where are we on getting Heard and Morales into custody?"

"Morales was picked up an hour ago," Marsh said. "Heard is still in Mexico, according to his passport. Robert Black, however, is on a plane to Munich."

"Fuck," Julia cursed. "Way to hide the ball, Nerd."

He raised both hands, palms out. "I already called Binny. The team there will be waiting for him when he lands."

"Levi," Sutton said, "what are you hiding up your sleeve?"

"Blaine's tidbit about his father's alias was a gold mine.

In addition to the embarrassing wealth of hotel receipts and at least two abortions Nathan White paid for, he also regularly conducts business with the Sanderses' undercover accounts."

"Keep going," Sutton said, his fist getting ever closer to the table. "I smell a conspiracy cooking, maybe even a RICO pie."

"As long as it's not Frito pie," Levi said, face scrunched.

"No Fritos, check."

Everyone around the table chuckled, Marsh included. He hoped like hell he and Levi got the chance to know Sutton better after this case. He was damn good at his job, and his mix of earnest integrity and dry wit was an intriguing combination. Marsh also sensed he and Levi would be fast friends, which was never a bad thing.

Levi nodded to Farmer, who flipped the on-screen display to a transaction record. "We're just starting to go through these and match them to dates and events, but that first payment to Sanders was made the day, during the last election cycle, when Anthony's opponent dropped out after being found in a motel room with drugs he still claims weren't his."

"And the deposits?"

"Two line up with Sixth Avenue Shelter funding," Matt said. "A third coincides with the latest defense spending bill."

Sutton's fist was inches from the table. "And the current case?"

"Light 'em up, Farmer," Levi said. Two of the transactions glowed yellow. "Two payments made to Robert Black. One last Thursday. The same amount last night."

Sutton's fist hit the table. "Pie for everyone!"

Everyone cracked up, but Levi apparently wasn't done. "Make that murder à la mode. Farmer, last line, please." A third line glowed. "And I believe that account belongs to one of the dead party crashers."

Marsh folded his arms on the table and buried his head in them, torn between laughing at Sutton and Levi and groaning at Stewart Anthony's appalling idiocy.

"He used the same alias?" Charlie sounded as baffled as he felt. "Every time?"

"Ego, man," Matt said. "Assholes like Anthony have enough money and connections to flee to a nonextradition country, but they stay, every fucking time. I will never understand."

"Did he really think he could be president with this many skeletons in his closet?" Julia asked.

Marsh lifted his head. "Remember what Stefan said. It was always a game. How far could he and Charles push each other and the world?"

"Please tell me this is enough to stop Anthony from pushing," Julia said to Sutton. "Sure looks like it to me."

"I know I'm only married to a US attorney," Cam said, "but I'm pretty sure even he would say this is enough."

"Me too," Sutton concurred, then said to Cam, "but if the federal prosecutor down here gives us any trouble, we might need your husband's help." He shifted his attention to Marsh and Levi. "We'll need Blaine's testimony, Catherine's too, and any other connections you can make between Anthony and his alias. At a minimum, it's enough to pick up Anthony and bring him in for questioning."

"Um," Julia said as she stared down at her phone. "I don't think we're going to need to pick Anthony up. He's here. With the sheriff's officers."

"Did *they* arrest him?" Alyssa said.

Matt was closest to the door. He spun out of his chair and yanked it open. Through the open door, Marsh spied Anthony across the floor at reception, a line of officers fanned out behind him. He wasn't in cuffs, though. "I don't think that's what's going on."

Their view was quickly eclipsed by Julia and Sutton, who exited first, Cam and Charlie on their heels.

Beside him, Levi shot into action. "Farmer, kill the screens and make sure you have everything backed up."

"Someplace private," Marsh added, and Farmer nodded. The screen went black the next second, his fingers flying over the keyboards.

"We gotta get the rest of this out of sight," Levi said as he began slapping folders closed.

They'd just shoved the last of them in boxes when Anthony was close enough for them to hear.

"Representative Anthony," Sutton said. "How can we help you?"

"You can turn around so Deputy Helms here can hand-cuff you."

"On what charges?" Julia asked, one hundred percent the SAC, that eerie calm that had served her well climbing the FBI ranks.

"Obstruction of justice and leaking classified informa-tion," Anthony said. "To start."

"Still trying to take the badge from me, Stewart?"

"Not trying anymore," Anthony said. "It's done." He swung his gaze to Levi, and the sheer evil there, mixed with barely concealed victory, made Marsh's stomach drop. "And so are you, Agent Bishop."

Marsh stepped closer to his husband, an arm around his

waist, as Julia and Matt moved more directly in front of them. "What for?" Cam asked as he joined the line of defense.

"The murders of Catherine Sanders and my son, Blaine Anthony."

"You've got to be kidding," Julia said over Matt's "Bullshit!"

"You don't look too broken up about losing your son," Charlie chipped in.

"It's not my first loss," Anthony said with not an ounce of the grief any good parent would be feeling.

Like the one who swayed heavily into Marsh's side, Levi's world no doubt spinning. "When exactly?" Marsh asked, failing at not raising his voice. "Levi's been with me since last night."

"Including that hour this morning when he visited Catherine Sanders?"

Levi sucked in a breath. "She was fine when I left. And I haven't seen Blaine since—"

"Don't," Marsh said, cutting him off. "Don't say anything else until Helena gets here."

Levi snapped his lips shut.

"I'd like a word with my husband," Marsh said. "Before you take him."

"Better make it count," Anthony said, the corner of his mouth twitching, fighting an evil smirk. "We never know when we might lose the ones we love."

Marsh stepped in front of his pale-as-a-ghost husband and gently guided him back into the war room. "Levi, baby, I need you to stash the panic I know you're feeling."

"How?" he croaked out.

"You need to be the agent who just solved this case. The

colleague who needs to have Sutton's back. And the father and husband who will come home to us tonight." Levi shook his head, disbelief and despair clouding his gaze. Marsh drew him into his arms, kissed his temple, and whispered the truth he'd only sorted in the last two minutes, a play that favored their side, that could deliver them the win once and for all. "Do you remember Hawes going dark at the party?" Levi nodded, his soft hair brushing Marsh's cheek. "I know—*we* know—who owns the last account Nathan White paid. You gotta let this play out." He knew he was asking a lot, but Levi was the strongest man he knew. He just needed a few hours to bring this home. And then he would bring Levi home too.

"Marsh, if something happens to me, David, he won't—"

"Nothing is going to happen to you." He framed his husband's cheeks, thumbs sweeping beneath the blue eyes he wanted to spend the rest of his days staring into. "I have your back. And so does our family. Do you trust us?"

"Completely," Levi answered with zero hesitation.

Marsh thanked him for that confidence with a kiss that reflected all the confidence he had in him too. Levi was strong, he was smart, and with their team and family behind them, they were going to win this game.

Tonight.

The king had been checked, and he didn't even realize it.

THIRTY

THE LOCK on the heavy lead door to the temporary holding cells turned, and Levi tensed where he was posted up on the back wall, hands clenched around either end of his unknotted tie. Chin down, he eyed the door through his lashes, waiting for it to open, to assess who was being led in. Prior to being escorted out for their phone calls, he and Sutton had been the only two detainees in this holding area reserved for prebooking intake. The cells were still empty when Levi returned from his call, but as the afternoon crept toward evening, that would change. For now, though, it was just Sutton returning from his phone call.

And looking like he'd been put through the wringer. His silver-streaked hair was a hand-raked mess, his broad shoulders slumped, his expression bone-deep weariness so full of sadness and regret that Levi's own chest ached. He waited for the officer to close the cell door behind Sutton, for Sutton to cross the room and lower himself onto the bench next to where Levi stood, for the big holding room door to close too before taking a seat beside him. "You look like you need that pie now?"

Eyes closed, Sutton leaned back against the cement wall and heaved a sigh. "I need all the pies."

"Your attorney go that hard on you?"

"Not my attorney, my ex." He raked his hands through his hair again, destroying any semblance of remaining order. "This goes the way I think it will, his name's going to be in the news again."

"The one who went to jail for your badge?"

He drew a knee up, heel braced on the bench, hands laced around his shin, and rested his forehead on his knee. "And now I'm going to lose it anyway."

"How do you figure? We're going to win this." Levi wasn't deterred, the borrowed cowboy confidence a powerful drug. "You'll be cleared, and Anthony will go to jail."

Sutton angled his head to cut a glare Levi's direction, a brow rising over one eye. "You seem more confident than you were an hour ago."

"Good call with my kid." He folded a knee up on the bench, leaned closer, and lowered his voice. "I also had time to process what my husband told me before we were led off in cuffs."

"Which was what exactly?"

He opened his mouth to tell Sutton about how Anthony had likely contracted the Madigans to kill Catherine and Blaine, foolishly thinking money and power would trump family because that's what he believed, except in this case he'd figured very wrong, but Levi cut himself short. His family was going to great lengths to protect him, venturing into the center of the board to make maneuvers in his and

Marsh's stead. He had to protect them too. *Trust.* That's what it all boiled down to, that's how Marsh made it work, how Levi would have to also make it work going forward because Marsh came with the Madigans, and Levi wasn't going to be without Marsh. "To trust him," Levi said instead, a shorter version of the truth.

Sutton wanted to question further, judging by the other raised brow and stern set of his jaw, the rulebook hardass he'd heard about making an appearance, but before he could get a word out, the lock flipped on the main door again.

Levi forced himself to maintain his casual posture, even as his muscles went tight, his nerves even tighter. Beside him, Sutton was similarly on guard, chin propped on his knee, the knuckles on the hands around his shin going white.

The door opened, and behind the guard trailed the two surviving party crashers. No disguising the menace in their eyes as the guard led them to the cell block two down from Levi and Sutton. No missing the guard "accidentally" dropping his keys close enough to the party crashers' cell for one of them to reach through and let themselves out.

To let themselves into Levi and Sutton's cell block.

"I've got eyes on them," Sutton muttered as soon as the door closed behind the guard. "What've we got for weapons?"

Levi scanned the room as discreetly as he could. "Not much." The benches were molded concrete, there were no windows, not even high transoms to break, no plumbing, fixtures, or beds, these cells only intended for short-term detention during processing. "Just the cameras, which aren't on." No recording light, no movement, no whirring noises. Weapons were all they were good for at this point. "Blunt objects and wires."

"How high up?"

Levi took another peek, estimated, and cringed. "Good twelve feet."

"That's out, then. So just the clothes on our backs."

"You've still got your tie and belt. You wearing your chain beneath your collar?"

Sutton nodded.

"I've got my tie and belt too," Levi said.

"Guards should've taken those from us."

"Payoff for always being polite whenever I'm down here."

Sutton's gaze flicked to the door. "Someone got paid more."

"Can't win 'em all."

Sutton's chuckle was cut short by movement two cells down, the taller one—Jason, if Levi recalled correctly—loping across the cell block, kneeling, and reaching an arm through for the keys. The shorter one—Brian—rose from the bench, his malicious gaze trained on Levi and Sutton.

"You can win them over," Sutton said, the claim so jarring Levi whipped his gaze to the SAC, who kept his on the approaching threats. "In the past week, you convinced Catherine to turn on her uncle and Blaine on his father. This should be a piece of cake."

"I thought we were talking about pie."

The corner of Sutton's mouth twitched, then leveled out as Jason unlocked the door to their cell.

As Sutton carefully moved a hand to his collar, starting to work his tie free, Levi stood with equal caution, his hand raised, palms out. "Jason, right?" he said to the taller of the two, meeting his blue eyes, then looked Brian in his brown eyes too. "And Brian? Can we talk about this?"

They stopped halfway across the holding cell, standing side by side, a bench between them and Levi and Sutton. "You killed Mike and Alex," Jason said.

"No," Levi said. "That was the person who hired you. He used you as cover."

"He hired us to do a job."

"That he had covered two other ways," Levi said as he heard Sutton rise behind him. As Brian's gaze tracked his every move. "You were expendable. You still are."

Sutton stepped to his side, tie dangling loose around his neck. "He killed the man he considered his father."

"His son too," Levi lied. "If he was willing to kill them, what do you think he'll do to you?"

Jason threaded his fingers through the keys on the ring, a sharp end poking out between each of his knuckles. "At least our families will be taken care of."

Brian lunged first, a foot on the bench between them, using it to launch himself Sutton's direction. Sutton ducked, spun under him, wrapped the tie around his back ankle and took him down in one swift move. Sutton yanked the tie back, wound either end around his hands, and lifted it in front of his face as a shield and weapon. The whole sequence was equal parts graceful and brawler.

Jason decided to try his chances with Levi instead. He took the less obstructed route, charging down the aisle between benches, directly at him. Levi juked one way, Jason corrected, and Levi spun the other to get behind Jason. Yanking free his tie, he held either end, whipped it over Jason's head, around his midsection, and yanked down and back hard. Jason rocked off-balance, and Levi flung him to the ground, where he collided with a groaning Brian.

"You're a brawler?" Levi asked Sutton as they squared up, blocking any exit for Jason and Brian, who were staggering to their feet.

"Contrary to popular belief, I wasn't born with the rulebook up my ass." He clenched the tie tighter and raised his fist higher as Jason and Brian righted themselves. "What's your excuse?"

"Jock," Levi answered as he pulled loose his belt. He wrapped the leather end around his wrist, metal buckle dangling free at the end for maximum damage. "And three older sisters."

"I can do this all day," Sutton said to their attackers, playing the bad cop.

"Or," Levi said, "you can take the deal we're offering you."

Jason started to lunge forward, but Brian's beefy arm shot out in front of him, putting a halt to his advance. "We'll take the deal," Brian said just as the cell block door was wrenched open.

Levi's eyes went to the white Stetson first. His husband's fiery brown eyes second. The icy blues of the woman beside him third. "What's this?" Helena said, and given the daggers in her voice, Levi could guess she'd been on the warpath for him all afternoon.

"More evidence." Levi snatched the ring of keys from where Jason had dropped them and tossed them through the cell bars to Marsh. "Is it over?"

Marsh unlocked the door and held it open for Levi and Sutton. "Catherine and Blaine just finished giving their statements."

Sutton's head whipped around so fast Levi almost laughed. "They're alive?"

Helena slammed the cell door shut and pocketed the keys. "Anthony solicited the wrong person to kill them."

Sutton split a look between them, no doubt a dozen questions warring on the tip of his tongue. He was SAC for organized crimes; the Madigans were on his radar. But he was also smart enough to know now wasn't the time to pick that fight, especially if he was on the way out the door. As if that realization had just dawned again, the earlier weariness crept back into his expression, sadness and regret muting everything else. He looped the tie back around his neck, cinching it unnecessarily tight. "I need to give a statement too."

Levi clasped his shoulder, sought to give the man who'd fought beside him, who'd helped him solve an impossible case, who'd buried himself inside the rulebook to hide from an age-old hurt, some comfort. "Maybe this is what you both need."

He nodded, then followed Helena out into the hallway. Marsh waited for Levi to exit, then shut the cell block door behind them. "We just need to get your things, and we can go." In the hallway, he pulled Levi into his arms, and Levi hugged him back through his shudders. "I told you you could do it."

Levi drew back enough to drop a kiss on the hinge of his jaw. "Not without you and our family."

"The prosecutor is ready to move on Anthony tonight. Do you want to be there when he's arrested?"

"I'd rather spend the evening at home."

Marsh brushed their lips together. "I couldn't agree more."

THIRTY-ONE

MARSH STOOD at the kitchen island, the sunset's glow and his family's laughter floating in through the back door and windows, the patio full for Sunday dinner. It was hard to believe that twenty-four hours ago Levi had been in lockup at the San Diego County jail. That after the falsified charges against him had been dropped and Marsh had brought him home, they'd fallen asleep last night on the couch during a *Dodgeball* rewatch with David, only to have their son excitedly wake them, his grin huge as he'd shoved his phone in their faces and shouted, "That asshole congressman from the valley is going to jail." Neither Marsh nor Levi had bothered to correct his language; it wasn't a lie. David had happy danced around the den, Taco barking up a storm, and Burrito taking cover under the couch.

Marsh, an arm around Levi's shoulder, had given him a squeeze and whispered in his ear, "You did that."

"*We* did that," Levi had corrected before snuggling closer and falling back to sleep in his arms.

There'd been some work calls that morning, some paperwork they'd had to run into the office to finalize and sign, but by noon, they'd been shopping at the farmers' market with his moms and David. They'd left with two flats full of goodies that had all been wiped clean at dinner, Levi coming through the door with a stack of empty dishes.

"They hated everything, huh?" Marsh teased as he scooped ice cream into coffee mugs.

"Especially the tomato, corn, and bacon hash." He set the plates in the sink and gave them a spray with the faucet. "Mom said it was the worst thing she's ever eaten."

"Then she's definitely not getting any of this horchata ice cream in her affogato. It's the worst."

Levi swiped the pint out from in front of him. "All mine."

"Hey!" Marsh grabbed him by a belt loop and dragged him back, his back colliding with Marsh's front. He snaked an arm around his waist and held him there, savoring the closeness, the freedom to hold his husband in his arms without the threat of the sky falling down around them. All that extra headspace and the gorgeous man in his arms led Marsh's mind in a singular direction. "You know what's the actual worst?"

Levi plucked the ice cream scoop from his other hand and continued filling cups where Marsh had left off. "What's that?"

Marsh palmed his ass with his newly free hand. "A house full of people when all I want to do is fuck my husband."

He appreciated the responsive shiver that rippled through Levi and raised goose bumps under his skin.

"Then let's finish preparing dessert so we can get them out of here."

"You really are the smartest man I know." Marsh dropped a kiss in the crook of his neck, sun and peppermint an enticing cocktail that threatened to keep him there, but he forced himself to unwind from around Levi and start up the espresso machine.

"You don't even like coffee," Marsh said, pausing before pouring coffee into the last waiting mug. "You could just eat the ice cream."

"And break my Italian mother's heart?" He poured a shot of amaretto into the mug on the opposite corner of the baking sheet he'd been using as a tray. "I'm a bad Italian. Don't tell anyone."

Marsh laughed, poured half an espresso shot into Levi's mug, then downed the other half. "Community property to the rescue."

They laughed as they finished loading the tray, Levi preparing to lift it when Marsh's phone pinged. He all but forgot the tray and stepped closer. "Is that work?"

Marsh dug the phone out of his pocket and opened the message from Helena, reading it aloud but also tilting the screen so Levi could see. "Catherine's being transferred to FCI Dublin."

"That's good news, right?"

Marsh nodded. "We've got eyes and ears there." Family and other Redemption assets they could trust to keep Catherine in line at the federal prison in the Bay Area. "We'll all be safe with her there."

Levi swayed on his feet, and Marsh nearly dropped his phone in his haste to get an arm around Levi and steady him. His forehead landed on Marsh's collarbone, and his torso rose and fell in heaving breaths under Marsh's hands. Marsh could guess what was going on in that head of his. Blaine was in protective custody. Anthony was being detained by the US Marshals and would be arraigned tomorrow in front of a judge who'd already told him not to waste the court's time requesting bail. Catherine's final resting place, so to speak, was the last play in the wind down of a dangerous six-week match that had taken them around the world and back.

That had brought them together and returned them home in one piece.

"We're good, baby," Marsh said as he coasted a hand up and down Levi's spine. "We're good."

A shuddery sigh later, Levi lifted his head, smile easy and bright even if there were tears in the corners of his eyes. "Sorry," he said, wiping away the wetness. "The relief just got to me there."

Relief. Marsh felt it too, all the way to his soul, and not just about the case. He knew where he wanted to be, who he wanted to be with, and for the first time, knew that feeling was one hundred percent mutual. He knew where he belonged, thanks to the beautiful man in his arms.

"Levi!" Margaret shouted from outside. "Where's my affogato?"

Levi laughed, the sound a little watery, and turned out of Marsh's arms toward the dessert tray. "Coming, Mom!"

Marsh intercepted him, clasping his hand and tugging him toward the patio door. "I think I know how to clear folks out of here."

"But the dessert—" Levi started.

Margaret finished his thought. "I don't see my affogato," she said as he and Levi stepped out onto the patio.

"I have something better," Marsh promised her, then shouted for David, who was in the far corner of the yard with his youngest cousin, picking flowers off the bushes to make a tiny bouquet. "David, can you come here? I need you for this too."

He handed Maddie off to her mother, then came to stand beside Levi, who was thoroughly confused judging by the deep divot between his brows. "Marsh, what—"

Until Marsh grasped his left hand in his and lowered onto one knee. Levi's eyes grew wide, his mouth falling open in a silent *Oh*, while David squeaked a "Holy shit" from beside him. Levi and Marsh corrected him together like the partners they'd become these past six weeks. Like the parent Marsh wanted to be.

He kept hold of Levi's hand but shifted his attention to David, speaking from the heart, knowing that his was the approval that mattered most to the man Marsh loved. "Would it be okay with you if I stuck around, if I loved your dad and you, if I continue to teach you chess and tell you to stop cursing even though I do it too?"

"Will you continue to make breakfast casserole every weekend?"

"Fuck yeah."

David's grin was even bigger than it had been last night, bigger even than the day the baby goats were born. "Then I'm good. You can stay."

Happy, muffled laughter erupted around them, except from the love of Marsh's life, who stood with his eyes closed, tears leaking out the corners and streaming down his face. Marsh would have been worried if not for the death grip Levi had on his hand. Marsh squeezed back. "Babe, open your eyes." He waited for those gorgeous blues to show themselves, for Levi to look love in the face again in front of his son and family. Marsh was the luckiest man alive to be that face, to be the person Levi had chosen. Who after having lost the first love of his life, he was willing to take a second, terrifying chance on. "This is the proposal you deserved, baby. In front of our family, in front of everyone who knows how brave you are and who loves you as much as I do. You gave me a home for my heart. Let me give you a heart to come home to, Levi, every fucking day, for as long as we have on this Earth. Levi Bishop, will you marry me?"

Levi hauled him up, into his arms and into everything Marsh had ever wanted. "In a fucking heartbeat."

THIRTY-TWO

MARSH'S PLAN DID NOT, in fact, get people out of their house sooner. Levi's arms were still around Marsh, their lips still locked, when the questions started to fly.

"When's the wedding?" his mom.

"Where's the wedding?" Marsh's mom.

"Where's the party?" Marsh's other mom.

David had all the answers. "Here at Christmas. They already promised."

A new round of affogato was required, then two bottles of champagne, and by the time the last glass was emptied, much of their impending wedding redo had been planned. Levi and Marsh answered questions when asked but otherwise let their family run with it. Hands entwined, they sat in the club chairs by the fire pit, enjoying the warm night, their elated family, and the promise of the future ahead of them. Together.

Levi would feel eyes on him every few minutes. He'd turn his head and catch Marsh staring, no care for who saw him gazing. Levi would stare right back until someone asked a question that required his or Marsh's input. The stares had started soft and affectionate, but as the night wore on, they grew heated, desire they'd been too tired to act on last night bubbling to the surface now. Levi tried to be patient in case Marsh was enjoying this, he'd never planned a wedding before, but when the topic of the guest list and Aunt Liz arose, Levi shot his sister Amy the SOS eyes he'd perfected as a kid.

"All right," Amy said with a clap. "I think we should leave the guest list to the grooms, who have plenty of time to nail that down."

"Not really," Margaret said. "It's only five months away."

"Plenty. Of. Time," Amy repeated, a line in the sand, the mirror image of their stubborn mother.

"Come on, M," Tom said as he offered her a hand up. "This is all code that our son and his husband-future-husband would like some alone time."

"Oh." Margaret giggled, then hopped to it but not without a detour by the fire pit. She kissed Marsh's cheek, then wrapped her arms around Levi's shoulders and kissed his cheek too. "You deserve this, baby boy. You deserve all the happiness in the world. I'm so glad you found it again."

Levi swallowed around the lump in his throat and patted his mother's hand. "Thank you, Mom."

"Do you want us to take David too?"

Levi grinned. "You're the best."

She winked. "I know."

It took another twenty minutes for everyone to clear out, including Marsh's moms who'd snagged a seaside room in Del Mar for their long-awaited nights by the coast.

Leaving Levi and Marsh truly alone.

Marsh pounced as soon as Levi closed the door behind their last guest, sandwiching him between the door and his big body. "Not my best plan ever." He trailed a line of nips and kisses down Levi's throat. "I've had better."

Levi threaded his fingers through Marsh's locks, the waves more voluminous by the day, long overdue for a cut, but Levi liked that he could curl his fingers in the strands and give them a tug. Loved the groan it elicited from Marsh. "Yes, it was a terrible plan for getting people out of our house." He tugged again, and Marsh lifted his face from where he'd buried it in the crook of Levi's neck. "But for making it a night—a proposal—I'll never forget, it was the best plan ever." He shifted and slid a leg between Marsh's. Lifted so his thigh was pressed tight to Marsh's taint. "You know what would make this the best night ever?"

Marsh ground down on his leg, his stiffening erection digging into Levi's hip. "I have an idea, but I want to hear you say it." He dragged his hands up Levi's torso, thumbs finding and flicking his nipples through his T-shirt. Body a live wire, Levi tipped back his head and groaned, his own hips thrusting for friction. "Tell me what you need, Levi. Ask for it."

Levi righted his head, confident enough now, thanks to the man in his arms, to ask for what he needed, to trust that his husband would give him what he wanted. "I need you to take me upstairs and tell me to stand naked in front of the window, my arms and legs spread, dick pressed against the glass. Then I want you to make me scream."

The teasing touches turned purposeful, Marsh's hands skating under his T-shirt, pushing it up and off. His mouth picking up where his fingers had left off, tongue swirling around his right nipple, flattening for a long swipe over it, teeth not so gently nipping. Repeating it all over again on the left. Then kissing a return path to his mouth, taking Levi apart with greedy lips, plundering strokes of his tongue, and deep rumbling groans that reverberated down Levi's throat.

It was almost enough to distract Levi from Marsh popping the button on his cargo shorts and sliding the zipper down. From slipping his hands inside the waist-band, palming Levi's ass cheeks, then pushing Levi's shorts and boxers over his hips, the fabric pooling around Levi's ankles.

Levi tore himself away from Marsh's mouth, panting as he leaned his head back against the door, then gasping as Marsh's fist closed around his cock. "Fuck, this isn't in front of the window. It isn't even upstairs."

Marsh chuckled, infuriating and sexy as hell. Levi attempted to swat at the hand that was doing wondrous things to his cock, but Marsh intercepted him and directed Levi's hand over the bulge behind his zipper. "In case you didn't notice, I'm already hard as a rock." He rocked his hips into Levi's palm. "Just watching you by the fire tonight, knowing I can do that every night for the rest of our lives, knowing you're willing to share all of you, all of this"—a long, slow stroke down Levi's cock—"with me, turned me the fuck on."

"Marsh, I need…"

"What do you need, baby?"

He righted his head and met those same fiery browns from over the fire pit earlier. "I need you to cowboy up.

Stop talking and put that tongue in my ass like you promised."

Marsh's grin was pure sin. It nearly melted Levi into a puddle, definitely made his knees weak, which made climbing the stairs a challenge. So did Marsh's arms around him, his clothed form at Levi's back, rough and delicious, his hands likewise rough and delicious as they wandered his front. It took entirely too long and entirely too much restraint, but they somehow made it to the bedroom.

The lamps and overheads were already off, the curtains and windows already open, just the moonlight casting the room in shadows and dim blue-gray light, the sounds of the bullfrogs and other wildlife echoing through the canyon. Levi stopped at the edge of the shadow by the nightstand where they'd ventured to retrieve the lube.

Behind him, Marsh slowed his questing hands, arms banding around Levi's torso. "We don't have to—"

"I thought I'd be more nervous," Levi admitted, then confessed the rest of the truth that was making his dick ache. "All I can think about is how warm that glass is going to feel, how good you're going to feel behind me, how much I want this—you—every day for the rest of my life too."

Marsh buried his face in his neck, muffling his "Jesus."

Smiling, Levi dropped a kiss on his temple. "Not Jesus. Just Levi."

Marsh lifted his face, smile easy and true, the one Levi had first seen on their wedding day, that he'd wanted to be the cause of every day since, including today. "Just perfect," Marsh said before capturing his mouth, slipping the lube from his hand, and getting them moving again.

The glass was warmer than Levi imagined, reminding him of slipping into a hot bath, but the only wetness in sight was the precome leaking from his cock, streaking the window, and Marsh's wet lips moving behind his ear. "Spread your legs and put your palms to the glass. Let those coyotes see who the wolf in this canyon is."

Warm all over, the glass in front of him, Marsh's big body behind him, the warmth—the love—that had wrapped itself around his heart. The heat that arrowed straight to his cock when Marsh slid down behind him, spread his cheeks, and speared his hole with his tongue. Levi leaned his forehead on the glass, staring at the vast canyon in front of him while his nerve endings threatened to burn him alive, while the rest of his world narrowed to the tongue that unrelentingly worked him over, to the lubed fingers Marsh pressed inside him too, exactly the way Marsh had promised.

Until Levi couldn't take it anymore, until he needed more, the rest of the fantasy Marsh had promised. He had no qualms asking for it any longer. He glanced over his shoulder as he pushed back with his ass, clenching enough to force Marsh's face out from between his cheeks. Levi nearly blew right then. Marsh's lips were wet, his beard wild, the blush on his cheekbones making his bronze skin glow, the dark pupils of his eyes blotting out the brown. Levi groaned and tipped his ass up. "I need your cock. Now." The sweetness with which Marsh kissed each ass cheek before he rose was Levi's undoing. "I love you. So fucking much."

Marsh cupped his face, a thumb under his eye, a smile turning up the corners of his lips. "I love you too, wolfy."

Levi laughed out loud, let it all go, let the coyotes and whoever was listening hear him. Let his husband see how much love and desire he had for him. "Fuck me, baby. Make it rough and messy."

Marsh kept his promises. Clothes still mostly on except for the jeans pushed down far enough to get his cock out, he slammed into Levi. Took him apart bit by bit. Sensation overload—the denim of his jeans rough against Levi's bare thighs, his T-shirted chest soft and warm against his back, his lips silky smooth on the nape of Levi's neck, whispering, "I love you," "You're beautiful," "I'm yours," "Everything." Words Levi repeated back along with *harder* and *please*. His emotions overloaded too—trust, freedom, happiness, love so big, so surprising, so welcome, so life changing. Like it was supposed to be. Like Levi never thought he'd have again.

Until a cowboy in a white Stetson swaggered into his life on the most improbable of nights. A night when Levi had been at his lowest. As he stared across the canyon now, stared across the past six weeks, he looked back on that night as the start of something unexpected and wonderful, of new highs. The start of a second chance for his heart. For love.

The windows rattled as they came together, now come-streaked and messy. But they held. Same as Levi's heart and body in Marsh's arms, where Levi trusted it would be forever safe. He'd keep Marsh's the same way. Would give him everything too. A home for the life and love—the heart —he'd entrusted to him.

———

For all the latest updates on new projects, sneak peeks, and more, sign up for Layla's Newsletter and join the Layla's Lushes Reader Group on Facebook.

———

Thank you for reading!

ACKNOWLEDGMENTS

Happy days for everyone, especially Marsh and Levi and their son David! It's always a lovely day when I get to send a happy fictional family out into the WhiskeyVerse and into readers hearts, even if it is a little bittersweet for me to finish their series. That said, as evidenced by this book full of WhiskeyVerse characters, I don't think it'll be the last you see of the Marshall-Bishop clan!

Thank you, readers, for your continued support of me, my stories, and these characters who live on in my heart too.

Thanks as well to the amazing team on *King Hunt*:

Cate Ashwood, Wander Aguiar, and Rodiney Santiago for another blazing hot cover. I love a sexy back shot!

Kim on beta, Susie Selva on edits, Lori Parks on proofreading.

Nina, the VPR Team, Leslie, and the GRR Team on publicity.

Christian Leatherman for continued excellent work narrating this series. I look forward to more projects in our future!

And finally all my love to the author friends, sprint partners, and cheerleaders who kept me going during a roller coaster of a fall and winter while drafting this book. I don't think I would have made it to the finish line without you!

ALSO BY LAYLA REYNE

For the most up-to-date list of titles and a helpful reading order, please visit www.laylareyne.com.

Over a Barrel

ABOUT THE AUTHOR

Layla Reyne is the author of *What We May Be* and the *Fog City, Perfect Play*, and *Table for Two* series. A Carolina Tar Heel who spent fifteen years in California, Layla enjoys weaving her bicoastal experiences into her stories, along with adrenaline-fueled suspense and heart pounding romance.

You can find Layla at laylareyne.com, in her reader group on Facebook—Layla's Lushes, and at the following sites:

- facebook.com/laylareyne
- twitter.com/laylareyne
- instagram.com/laylareyne
- bookbub.com/authors/layla-reyne

Ingram Content Group UK Ltd.
Milton Keynes UK
UKHW021845140623
423431UK00014B/287

9 798986 922904